THE AFGHAN

A Joe Johnson Thriller

ANDREW TURPIN

The Write Direction Publishing

First published in the U.K. in 2019 by The Write Direction Publishing, St. Albans, U.K.

Copyright © 2019 Andrew Turpin
All rights reserved.
The Afghan print edition
ISBN: 978-1-78875-010-3

Andrew Turpin has asserted his right under the Copyright, Designs and Patents Act 1988 to be identified as the author of this work.

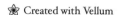 Created with Vellum

WELCOME TO THE JOE JOHNSON SERIES!

Thank you for purchasing *The Afghan* — I hope you enjoy it!

This is a prequel to the series of thrillers I am writing that are set in the present day and feature **Joe Johnson**, a US-based independent war crimes investigator.

The Afghan, however, is set back in 1988, when Johnson worked for the CIA in Pakistan and Afghanistan. He later also worked for the Office of Special Investigations — a section of the Department of Justice responsible for tracking down Nazi war criminals hiding in the United States.

The other books in the series about his various war crimes investigations are all for sale on Amazon. In order, they are:

Prequel: *The Afghan*
1. *The Last Nazi*
2. *The Old Bridge*
3. *Bandit Country*
4. *Stalin's Final Sting*
5. *The Nazi's Son*

If you enjoy this book, I would like to keep in touch. This is not always easy, as I usually only publish a couple of books a year and there are many authors and books out there. So the best way is for you to be on my Readers Group email list. I can then send you updates on the next book, plus occasional special offers.

If you are not already in my Readers Group and would like to receive the email updates, you can sign up at the following link and I will send you a free taster ebook boxset containing the first few chapters of the other books in the series:

https://bookhip.com/DGWGVP

If you only like paperbacks, you can still just sign up for the email list at the link above.

Or a full ebook boxset of the first three books in the series is available on Amazon at a discount. Just type "Andrew Turpin Joe Johnson Thriller Series" into the Amazon search box and you can't miss it!

Andrew Turpin

This book is dedicated to the estimated two million Afghans who died during the Soviet occupation of their country from 1979-1989.

"The Stinger changed everything and we were no longer scared. We could knock that Hind out of the sky at will. Before that US missile arrived, we hardly ever won a set-piece confrontation with the Soviets. After it arrived we never lost one."

Mohammed Gulab, Pashtun warrior, quoted in *The Lion of Sabray*, by Patrick Robinson, published by Touchstone (2015).

PROLOGUE

Saturday, January 2, 1988
Khost-Gardez Pass, southeastern Afghanistan

Javed Hasrat heard them before he saw them. The muffled and distant clattering of the Russian helicopter gunship engines echoed across the valley. The sound bounced off the semi-vertical boulder-strewn slopes rising more than three hundred meters on either side of the river that twisted along like a white ribbon to his left.

Then came the distant, pulsing rat-at-tat-tat of machine gun fire, accompanied by the whoosh of rockets. A few seconds later there was an explosion and from out of sight, behind an outcrop that jutted out toward the river and the dirt road next to it, rose a cloud of gray smoke.

"Bastards, they've hit Wazrar," Javed said in his native Pashto, his voice suddenly cracked and reedy. He tugged at his long black beard and stared east, but from his current vantage point, he was unable to see the village and its collec-tion of mud-brown houses, where he knew his family and others would now be cowered, probably under tables or anything else that might offer protection. "Baz, get it ready, in case they head this way."

Baz, one of the three men standing next to Javed, shook his head. "They won't. They'll head back to Gardez."

"Get it ready anyway," Javed said. He knew that Baz was probably right. The Russians were currently in a phase of hit-and-run activity that involved them swooping in, destroying as much of a village as they could from the air, then exiting swiftly to avoid casualties from mujahideen fire.

The attacks had been going on for weeks, ever since the Soviets launched Operation Magistral to gain control of the pass, in the southern part of the Hindu Kush mountain range. It was a vital supply artery that connected Kabul to the north with Khost, to the southeast, where there was a large Russian military base. Beyond that, the pass was a link to Pakistan and India.

Javed felt proud that the mujahideen had controlled the pass since the Soviet invasion of 1979. But during December, the Soviet 40th Army, coming in from Gardez in the north, had used thousands of troops and sheer brute force to regain control of it and finally opened up the route to Khost.

Now the Russians were launching periodic forays, both airborne and on the ground, against mujahideen bases and villages to ensure that the pass remained open and they retained control.

Baz, wiry and with forearms that seemed to be hewn from lengths of steel rope, bent and picked up the one-and-a-half-meter matte green missile that lay next to him in the snow, then handed it to Javed.

Javed raised the Stinger so it rested on his right shoulder, its long tube stretched out behind him. He applied his eye to the chunky sight mounted on the front and swung the weapon toward the right side of the outcrop of rock, behind which the attack on the village had taken place.

Really, the arrival of the Stingers, supplied seemingly out of nowhere by the Americans, had been a gift from Allah in their battle against the Russians, he thought.

Then the four men waited.

Baz was wrong. Twenty seconds later three wasp-like Mil Mi-24 attack helicopters—Hinds, as the Americans called them—flying in a V formation, rounded the rock outcrop. Their outlines, with twin rocket launchers hanging beneath their stub wings, were clearly visible against the snow-covered backdrop of the stark mountainside behind them.

Javed stared at the helicopters. Rather than heading back to base in Gardez, the choppers were flying in the opposite direction—which based on previous experience, could mean only one thing: they were intending to take out the next village along the valley too.

"I'm going to have them," Javed said.

The helicopters moved steadily toward them, now more clearly visible against a clear blue sky. They tracked up the river and the tortuously winding rough dirt road of the Khost-Gardez Pass that ran alongside it.

Javed began the now well-grooved process of preparing his beloved Stinger for firing. He bent down and picked up the small, round battery coolant unit—a thermal battery that provided power for the infrared tracking device and argon gas to keep it cool. He screwed it into the base of the gripstock, then returned the weapon to its position on his shoulder.

He placed his right index finger on the trigger, his left hand underneath the front of the FIM-92 Stinger. Behind him, one of the other men, Sandjar Hassani, checked that the weapon was aligned correctly.

Javed lined up the leading Mi-24 in his sight, lifted the device and activated it against the blue sky by pressing the safety and actuator switch, then realigned it with the chopper. There was an audible tone as the Stinger's infrared mechanism locked onto its target, and Javed pressed the uncage button at the front of his weapon, which allowed it to automatically track the helicopter.

Then, using the sight, he elevated the tube a little to compensate for the effect of gravity and slowly pulled back the trigger. After another couple of seconds there was an explosion as the launch motor ignited, ejecting the missile from its launch tube several meters out in front of Javed before the main flight motor kicked in with a deafening whoosh.

"Allahu akbar!" Javed shouted. "Allahu akbar!"

The four men watched, almost mesmerized, as the Stinger, trailing a white line of gases across the blue sky, curved toward the lead Hind at more than seven hundred meters per second, its infrared detector locked onto its target's engine and exhaust heat.

The Hind burst into an orange and yellow fireball, throwing off chunks of debris, then hung in the sky momentarily, as if defying gravity, before plunging almost vertically into the river below with a huge explosion that threw up a cloud of black smoke.

Javed saw immediately that one of the other two helicopters was also in deep trouble. Maybe it had been hit by debris from the first. It fell sharply, spinning a little, and then the pilot appeared to regain control, bringing it to perhaps twenty meters above the ground before it plunged onto the highway with a loud crash and the squeal of tortured metal. However, the aircraft didn't explode.

"Dakh-rā zoya!" Baz said. "Son of a donkey."

Javed's face remained grim, in stark contrast to his usual reaction upon hearing his friend's favorite expression. He took a couple of steps forward, his feet half covered by several centimeters of snow, and peered up the valley. "Praise Allah. We got two with one hit, Baz," he said. "Now let's go and see if any of the bastards in those choppers are still alive. If they are, we'll take them back to the village and show them the damage they've done before we finish them off."

PART ONE

CHAPTER ONE

Wednesday, February 3, 1988
Langley, Virginia

Joe Johnson glanced across at his colleague Vic Walter, who sat with arms folded tight across his chest. They were perched at opposite ends of a long leather sofa in the director of central intelligence's office on the seventh floor of the CIA's Langley headquarters.

In an armchair on the other side of a coffee table sat their boss, Robert Watson, chief of station in Islamabad, where they were all based. The three men had been due to head to Dulles Airport two hours earlier for their return flight to the Pakistani capital, following a routine visit to base. But instead, they were summoned by a call from the director Alfred Meyer's executive assistant.

Two Democratic senators had hurriedly arranged briefings with Meyer, wanting more details on the now enormous US budget for the Afghanistan program, designed to support the mujahideen in their battle against the occupying Russian forces. The duo, along with several of their colleagues in the Senate, had opposed the budget allocation, approved only a few weeks earlier. This was because most of the money was being distributed via Pakistan, which to the concern of the United States government was known to be developing nuclear weapons.

Meyer wanted Watson and his Islamabad-based team on the ground to help explain in detail to the senators exactly what the money was being used for and why the program was critical. Both Johnson, who had only encountered the director once before, and Walter were surprised to be invited along.

The executive assistant, a tall woman with a black bob, emerged from the director's conference room and beckoned them. "You can come in now. They're ready," she said.

Watson, an angular forty-two-year-old, stood and fixed first Johnson, then Walter, with a stare. "You two just sit and listen and say nothing unless you're spoken to, understand?"

They nodded and followed Watson into the conference room.

There, sitting on the left side of a long oval birch table, was Meyer. On the right were the two senators, Simon Rudder and Tony Kendall, both dressed almost identically in white shirts, ties, and navy suits.

Penguins, Johnson thought, running his hand through his short-cropped and slightly receding dark hair. He knew that both of them had already argued strongly to stop all aid to Pakistan, and thereby to Afghanistan, given that the Pakistanis controlled all flows of money and arms to the mujahideen. This opposition followed the discovery the previous summer that an agent for General Zia-ul-Haq, the Pakistan president, had been in the US attempting to buy tons of a special type of steel vital to construction of a nuclear weapon.

It would be interesting, Johnson thought, to see how Meyer deflected the senators' likely onslaught, since that the CIA had been the below-radar driver behind the supply of hundreds of millions of dollars' worth of weapons to the mujahideen—US funding in 1987 had topped $630 million, up from just $20 million in 1980. Only Egypt and Israel were getting more American cash.

The only reason the funding had been approved by the joint House-Senate Appropriations Conference Committee was because of the herculean efforts of Congressman Charlie Wilson, who had championed the cause of the mujahideen. Wilson had persuaded his colleagues on the House Defense Appropriations Subcommittee to ramp up the Afghan budget year after year.

It was Wilson who had been largely responsible for the most notable addition to the weaponry supplied to the mujahideen—Stingers. These lethal handheld, heat-seeking ground-to-air missiles had over the previous eighteen months wreaked havoc among the Russian helicopter and fixed-wing aircraft fleets operating across Afghanistan.

Even before the trio had taken their seats, Meyer got right to the point. "I've explained our strategic goals for Afghanistan—about the need to finish the job, and the geopolitical threat to the States and globally if Russia isn't finally driven out, that they could simply overrun the region and threaten Pakistan and eventually the Persian Gulf," he said.

Meyer turned to Watson. "Now, tell the senators exactly what you're seeing in the villages."

Watson cleared his throat. "Frankly, it's nothing short of genocide," he said, running his fingers through his salt-and-pepper hair. "We think about three million refugees are living in about three hundred makeshift camps along the Pakistan-Afghanistan border. They're dying by the thousands—disease is rife, and there's nowhere near enough clean water and food. The Soviets have literally shot them out of their homes with their Hinds—they've used those choppers to turn it into a goddamn turkey shoot. And it's still going on. So if we don't keep the weapons flowing, especially the Stingers, they'll keep on doing it."

Rudder didn't change his expression. Clearly he wasn't going to be moved by humanitarian tales of woe. The senator glanced at Kendall, then directed his gaze back to Watson.

"In that case," Rudder said, "you need to make damn sure you've got more control over where the weapons are going to. I'm not saying this, of course, but there's no point for us being in Afghanistan unless we get more dead Russians. And if you can't be sure that the Pakistanis are going to achieve that, then you need to grab more control of the weapons distribution process yourselves. Make your own arrangements with the mujahideen."

"We think the ISI has good systems in place," Watson said. "They know who they're distributing to. But you're right —we do need more control and we're working on that, don't worry. We're talking to the British about how we can work below the Pakistanis' radar to improve things."

"If you don't have control," Rudder said, tapping his fingers on the table for emphasis, "my worry is where all those weapons are going. Who's to say the mujahideen aren't going to sell them to terrorist groups—maybe anti-American ones?"

"I don't think that's going to happen," Watson said.

"But how do you know?" Rudder persisted. "Where's the inventory of who's taking what and what they're doing with it?"

Seemingly unsure about how to respond to a question about such highly classified details, Watson looked to Meyer, who said, "We've got that in hand, Simon. I'm not at liberty to tell you how, but I can assure you it's all under control."

Rudder shook his head. "And while on the subject of Hinds," he said, "from what I understand, you haven't even captured a single one intact yet. Neither have you managed to get a Soviet communications van. Isn't it critical to do that?"

He raised his eyebrows at Watson, whom Johnson could see was visibly struggling to restrain himself. The Agency had been actively trying for some time to do exactly what Rudder was talking about. The intelligence value for both the Afghan program and the wider Cold War would be enormous.

Johnson stroked the dark beard he had grown since his arrival at the Islamabad station in June 1986. How would Watson get out of that question?

But what his boss said next caused Johnson's jaw to drop.

"We've got that under control, actually," Watson said to Rudder. "We know the importance of that. In fact, my colleague here, Joe Johnson, is running an operation to pull in both a Hind and a comms van. He's taken responsibility for the project and is quite advanced with his planning."

What? Johnson thought. *Capture a Hind and a comms van? The bastard has to be kidding.* It was the first he had heard of it. True, the office as a whole had discussed possible ways of trying to secure both pieces of Russian technology. But Johnson had been little more than a bit-part contributor to the discussions. His main job as a case officer in Islamabad had been something different: to develop sources among the Pakistani intelligence service, the ISI.

Johnson had never liked his boss. Watson had proved himself to be a shifty, highly political, untrustworthy operator who never hesitated to take credit for others' work and to stab colleagues in the back if he felt the need to divert the blame for mistakes away from himself.

Now, in front of the director and two high-ranking senators, Johnson—aged twenty-nine and with less than three and a half years at the CIA—had been dropped deep in the shit. He glanced at Vic, who was fiddling with his metal-rimmed glasses, clearly also irritated.

"Okay, that's good to know," said Rudder. "You'll need to get a move on, though, young man," he added, staring at Johnson. "We've got a meeting with members of the Senate Defense Appropriations Subcommittee during the second week of April. If you haven't got the job done by then, that'll be the end of your Afghan program if I have anything to do with it. We'll be discussing the budget for the fiscal year starting in October, and there's a lot of senators thinking the way I'm thinking." He stared at Watson, then Johnson and Vic in turn. "Understood?"

Johnson nodded, noticing out of the corner of his eye that although Meyer was already launching into a defense of the Afghan budget, the director of the Central Intelligence Agency was looking straight at him.

CHAPTER TWO

Saturday, February 6, 1988
Khost-Gardez Pass

The convoy of four mules, accompanied by three men, wound its way slowly up the lightly snow-covered mountain path in single file. The glare from the sun on the snow caused the man leading the group to squint a little as he stopped for a breather at the top of a steep incline.

Javed Hasrat was still coming to terms with the shock he had experienced more than a month earlier. That was when he had been told that the Hind helicopter attack on Wazrar had decimated the village, reducing his house to a smoking ruin and killing his wife, Ariana, and youngest daughter, Hila, only eight years old.

He, Baz, and Sandjar had arrived at the wreckage of the Russian helicopters to find two other men from his village waiting there to give him the tragic news.

A red mist of hatred had rapidly encompassed him. The crew of the helicopter that had taken a direct hit from the

Stinger had all died, but those in the second chopper that had crash-landed had been fully conscious, and they had taken the full force of Javed's anger. He had ensured they suffered greatly before finally meeting their end.

It was only after the deed was done that he sank to the ground and wept for his lost family members.

At thirty-eight, he had felt as though he had aged another three decades. He had gone into a deep depression that had only begun to lift thanks to the love and resilience shown by his two surviving older daughters, Roshina and Sandara, aged sixteen and fourteen, respectively.

Javed put his hand up to his face to shield his eyes and studied Baz, standing next to him, and Baz's younger brother, Noor.

"Nearly there. Another kilometer," Javed said. He straightened his traditional pale gray linen *shalwar kameez*—baggy trousers and a long shirt—and adjusted his jacket and *chitrali* cap. The action was unnecessary, an almost unconscious habit that he had developed as a youngster.

He gazed along the path ahead of them, which narrowed sharply and turned into little more than a two-meter-wide ledge carved into the face of the cliff.

The mules all had tarps covering the loads on their backs. Javed certainly didn't want anyone to see what was underneath. The animals were each carrying four FIM-92 Stingers on their backs, all wrapped in clear plastic sheeting, packed into special canvas holders, and disguised under packages of food and blankets.

It was the only way to transport the weapons, weighing about fifteen kilograms each, from Wazrar, on the Khost-Gardez highway, to the safety of the cave, about ten kilometers northeast of the village in the Sulaiman Mountains. No vehicle could navigate the tortuous route.

Following the downing of the two Hinds, the Russians had continued to mount occasional attacks on the villages.

But the mujahideen commanders had noticed that over the past week, these attacks had dwindled sharply in frequency, and there were rumors that the Soviet troops were withdrawing.

For Javed this had been no consolation. He ached with the loss of his wife and daughter and doubled his determination to take every opportunity possible to exact revenge on the Russians.

It was for that reason that he had decided to move sixteen of the Stingers under his control to the safety of the cave, leaving just five in a weapons cache near the pass itself for quick access if required. He was concerned that if the Russians really were leaving, his precious Stingers might be stolen by rival mujahideen commanders. Or maybe the Americans who had supplied them might try to claw them back. He might need them for another day and couldn't risk them disappearing.

He had already moved two shoulder-fired RPG-7 rocket-propelled grenade launch tubes, plus six grenades, to the cave four days earlier for the same reason. That left him with two launch tubes and ten grenades in the pass.

The convoy moved on up the path, now traveling with extreme care given the sheer vertigo-inducing drop of more than a hundred meters that lay over the ledge to their right.

Half an hour later, they stood under a rock overhang, beneath which was the entrance to a natural cave in the cliff face, concealed behind a fissure in the rock surface. The overlapping shape of the fissure and the overhang ensured that the cave entrance was virtually invisible to anyone not in the immediate vicinity and certainly undetectable from the air. The cave had been discovered by one of the other villagers from Wazrar while he had been searching for some lost sheep, and he had mentioned it to Javed.

As he had done during the entire journey up from the pass, Javed checked carefully all around the area for any sign of surveillance. There was nothing.

Then he took the lead mule behind the rock and into the cave beyond. The others followed. Javed switched on a small flashlight and used it to locate three kerosene lamps hidden behind a rock.

Once he had lit the lamps, the interior of the cave became visible. It was a naturally occurring space that could almost have been custom-designed. High-ceilinged, it stretched at least thirty meters back from the entrance and was more than twenty meters wide. At the rear was another fissure, almost a narrow doorway, that led to another smaller cavity beyond, where the weapons were stored on a ledge above head height and out of sight of any intruders.

"Let's get this lot unloaded, quickly," Javed said, twirling his forefinger rapidly in circles in front of him, indicating the need for speed.

Baz leaned against one side of the mule at the front of the convoy while Noor, who was two years younger at thirty-six, leaned against the other side. Both brothers seemed in less of a rush.

"I've heard that Royan has got hold of another twenty Stingers and several multiple-barrel rocket launchers," Baz said. "And Salar got fifteen Stingers."

Royan, one of relatively few Tajiks in the predominantly Pashtun Sulaiman ranges, was a rival mujahideen commander in the neighboring valley and was known to be exceptionally wealthy. He and Javed had dropped their historically bitter tribal enmity in the interests of defeating a common enemy— Russia—and ensuring a flow of American weapons. But if the Russians really were going, Javed knew it wouldn't be long before the status quo—traditional hostilities between tribes —would be resumed.

Salar was a Pashtun mujahideen commander, based slightly farther north, who was a strong ally and friend of Javed and Baz. There had been a long-standing relationship between their tribes, based on alliances during past conflicts and occasional intermarriages between families.

"Where did they get them from?" Javed asked.

"That's a good question," Baz said. "I know for sure it wasn't from the ISI."

Inter-Services Intelligence, the Pakistani intelligence agency, had managed the delivery of the entire stock of weapons and ammunition supplied by the CIA to the Afghan mujahideen, on the insistence of President Zia, who refused to allow the Americans to deal with them directly.

"So who, then?" Javed asked.

"Two Americans," Baz said. "I know that for sure."

Javed's eyes narrowed. "Direct from Americans?"

Baz nodded. "Yes." He rubbed his right thumb and forefinger together, as if wrinkling banknotes. "Someone's making a lot of money."

"Do you know who?" Javed asked.

"I don't know names, but I do have a copy of a photo my good friend Mehtar took of the Americans delivering the Stingers. He's one of Salar's men."

"I know Mehtar. Why did he give you a photo?"

"He asked me to keep it safe for him—as a backup. He trusts me. He said it was in case the Americans played dirty."

CHAPTER THREE

Monday, February 8, 1988
Islamabad

It didn't take long. Johnson and Vic had only been back in Islamabad for less than a day when they were called in to Robert Watson's office in the CIA station on the third floor of the United States embassy.

The embassy, rebuilt after being torched by marauding Islamic protesters in 1979, now housed a somewhat generic collection of office suites, like any other government office in the world.

Johnson and Vic made their way to a meeting room at the far end of the corridor, where Watson and his deputy chief of station, Alec Jameson, were waiting. Neither Johnson nor Vic had had an opportunity to speak with Watson after the meeting the previous week in Langley with the two senators and Director Meyer, and they had traveled back to Islamabad separately from their boss.

Now they sat down opposite Watson, who leaned forward, his arms folded on the table, tieless, but with his shirtsleeves neatly fastened with gold cuff links.

"Let's start with that meeting last Wednesday," Watson said. "I meant what I said, and that damned senator unfortunately meant what *he* said too. We need to make sure more weapons go to the right muj commanders—the objective is to kill more Russians, but we can't have our fingerprints on the job sheet."

He looked at Johnson and raised an eyebrow. "So, I want you to join the meetings with MI6."

Watson was referring to the small team of three from the CIA station that met twice weekly with counterparts from the British Secret Intelligence Service, otherwise known as MI6, to exchange information and explore ways of jointly working together.

Until now, Johnson hadn't been involved in the MI6 meetings. However, he knew the Brits were in practice less constrained than the CIA in arranging operations that might end in the deaths of Russians. There were fewer lawyers crawling over everything they did, for a start.

MI6 also often had better connections among the mujahideen, to whom they were already channeling weapons. What the British definitely didn't have was money or equipment—for example, mine detectors for their Afghan drivers to use—and that was where the CIA could help.

"Where do you want us to focus?" Johnson asked, fingering his beard.

"Khost-Gardez Pass, for a start," Watson said. "We need to disrupt the Russians there as much as possible. And then the Panjshir Valley."

Both passes were highly strategic. The Panjshir, around forty-five miles north of Kabul, was a key route for the

Russian truck convoys bringing supplies to the 40th Army in Afghanistan. The mujahideen commander Ahmad Shah Massoud had been ferocious in ambushing any Russian attempt to take the valley, although the Soviets had dramatically reduced the number of offensives there in the past couple of years.

Watson eyeballed Johnson. "Also, I want you to get us a Hind and a comms van. We can't afford to upset those senators—if they start lobbying to pull the plug on the Afghan program our work here is screwed. I also want you to start finding more sources in the muj and the ISI so we can track where all the weapons we're supplying are going to. Who's getting them and what's happening to them. Right?"

Johnson felt sorely tempted to confront Watson for ambushing him at Langley the previous week, but he decided to let it go. "So Meyer's caved in to Rudder, then, has he?" Johnson asked.

"Seems so. You heard Rudder," Watson said. "He thinks if the Russians end up leaving Afghanistan, then great, job done. But all this firepower's going to be left with the muj, and God knows what they'll do with it."

This seemed like the shortest of short straws to Johnson. Every piece of equipment and weaponry and all the vehicles that the US had supplied via the ISI had vanished into a mujahideen maze and had been siphoned off into the mountains by any number of tribal groups. Trying to track where everything was going would be a damn near impossible task.

"Okay," Johnson said. "I don't think we're going to do any more than scratch the surface, but I'll do what I can. How much can I pay the muj?"

"You can pay a retainer—twenty grand a month, up to fifty for a muj commander who's got an overview across one or two provinces. Just don't let the ISI know what you're doing. Tradecraft has to be 100 percent."

Johnson fell back in his chair. Even twenty grand a month was several multiples of what he was earning as a US government employee.

Jameson, a thin-faced, dark-haired man in his late forties, chipped in. "We want to get to Rostov too—either recruit him or disable him."

As everyone in the CIA station was aware, Leonid Rostov, a notorious former sniper with the Red Army, was now the number two in Afghanistan in Line PR, the KGB's division responsible for military intelligence operations and active measures. He effectively directed the military arm of the Afghan intelligence service, the KHAD, which was firmly under KGB control.

It was Rostov's advice and say-so that governed Russia's helicopter gunship attacks on villages and other tribal positions. Because of this, Johnson could see exactly where Jameson was coming from.

"Chances of recruiting Rostov have to be close to zero," Johnson said.

Jameson nodded. "Yep. So . . . disable him."

Johnson had previously heard Jameson say that recruiting Russians was a waste of time and killing them was far more productive. Of course, he didn't mean doing it personally—he would get the mujahideen to do it for him.

"Do we have any pictures of Rostov?" Johnson asked.

Jameson reached inside a cardboard file and handed Johnson a black-and-white photograph, which he studied. Rostov had a wide face with a couple of jowls and a mop of black hair that was combed backward.

Johnson handed the photo back and decided not to comment further on the issue of killing Russians. This was dangerous territory. Since he joined the CIA's Islamabad station, he had learned not to poke his head too far above the parapet on certain issues, and this was one of them.

Privately, Johnson felt that lethal force should be deployed on an as-needed basis rather than for the sake of it. Setting out to kill a KGB agent would be far more likely counterproductive than helpful.

But Watson ran his station in a highly political way, and Johnson never felt confident that any comment he might make wouldn't later be used against him.

It had taken some getting used to. Johnson had grown up in the small city of Portland, on the Maine coast, the son of a father with British ancestry and a Polish-Jewish immigrant mother, Helena, who survived two years in the Gross-Rosen concentration camp during the Second World War. She had instilled in Johnson a deep awareness of justice, a sympathy for persecuted ethnic minorities, and a determination to try to do some good in the world.

After the meeting with Watson and Jameson, Johnson walked with Vic back to their own office, where they worked alongside their colleague Neal Scales, also a case officer.

"What d'you think, Doc?" Vic asked. He had wasted no time in giving Johnson the nickname because of his PhD on the economics of the Third Reich that he had completed at the Freie Universität in Berlin, completed during the four years prior to joining the CIA in 1984, when he was twenty-six.

"He's picking on me because I speak Pashto better than him," Johnson said. "It's a no-win situation."

"You're right there. I know who you could start with, though—MILLPOND."

MILLPOND was the cryptonym for Haroon Rashid, an ISI officer whom Vic had begun cultivating but had recently started to hand over to Johnson because Vic had been reassigned to work linked to Pakistan's nuclear program. MILLPOND had good connections with various high-level mujahideen commanders inside Afghanistan.

Johnson nodded. "Yeah, I had him in mind."

"You just need to be damn careful, though," Vic said. "The ISI are running surveillance on everyone who breathes in this station."

CHAPTER FOUR

Tuesday, February 16, 1988
Islamabad

Yuri Severinov walked swiftly through Jinnah Market, past the jumbled array of jeweler's shops, snack bars, bookshops, and gadget retailers toward the safe house, where he was due to hold his fourth scheduled meeting with his new American source, whom he had code-named TENOR.

The first meeting, initiated by TENOR three months earlier through a mutual contact, had come as a considerable surprise to Severinov. It was the first time he had received such an approach by an American, and he had begun by treating the man with the utmost caution—not least because he worked for the CIA.

It was unclear what his motives were and also whether he would deliver anything of value.

But at the second meeting in mid-December, TENOR had moved the process along quickly. First, he proved his credibility by providing a valuable list of mujahideen commanders to whom he said the ISI had delivered weapons, including Stingers, rocket-propelled grenades, and multibarrel rocket launchers. All the weaponry was intended for use against the occupying Russian forces, the 40th Army. There were some well-known names on the list, which looked entirely plausible. It all checked out.

A deal with TENOR was rapidly arranged, with payments in dollars into his numbered bank account in Zürich in exchange for further information.

To Severinov, as a hard-nosed officer in the KGB's Line PR unit, it seemed like an opportunity for a quick win. And quick wins were something he was always on the lookout for —a mind-set instilled in him by his father, Sergo, who had spent seven years working for Josef Stalin from 1945 until 1952. Sergo's favorite saying was inscribed in a framed quotation he had given to Yuri: "Be a bee that stings for the Motherland: be busy, be dangerous." It summed him up.

Now, though, the time frame to achieve a quick win from TENOR was short. It was obvious that the Soviet Union was going to pull its troops out of Afghanistan later that year. Indeed, Soviet leader Mikhail Gorbachev had said as much the previous week. So Severinov needed to move quickly; if he could do so, here was a chance to get some valuable credit with his immediate boss, Leonid Rostov.

A rising tide floats all boats, Severinov thought to himself, running a hand through his short, wiry black hair. And there had been few Russian successes during the disastrous Afghan occupation.

If Severinov could supply his boss with intelligence from TENOR that led to successful attacks on mujahideen bases, the killing of muj commanders, and the recovery of weapons that might otherwise be used against the retreating Russian troops, it could earn promotions for both of them once the withdrawal process was completed.

The trick, of course, would be to ensure that Rostov's superior at the Lubyanka in Moscow, Anatoly Yurenko, knew who had done the real work.

Severinov, a tall, well-muscled thirty-one-year-old, completed his surveillance detection routine, which had taken him more than an hour. Certain that he had no coverage from the ISI, CIA, or anyone else, he carefully entered the apartment block just off Bhittai Road, in Islamabad's F-7 sector. It seemed an oasis of quiet after the raucous bustle of the market.

He climbed the bare concrete stairs to the second floor, his footsteps echoing down the stairwell, and let himself into the safe house, a lightly and cheaply furnished two-bed apartment, acquired by the KGB the previous year.

It was difficult for the KGB to operate in Islamabad, given hostility in the country to the Afghan occupation. Nobody was going to do any Russian a favor. The least worst option for Severinov and Rostov was to travel using false identities as employees of Aeroflot, the Russian airline, which had offices in the city. It gave them a good excuse to be in town. The apartment, meanwhile, was rented in the name of a nonexistent airline human relations manager.

Normally, Severinov would manage this type of meeting alone. But for a source of TENOR's standing, Rostov had wanted to join, as he had the previous two occasions.

Severinov made himself a strong coffee and sat on the sofa to wait.

Ten minutes later, there was a double knock at the door, followed by a triple knock. That was Rostov's signal. He opened the door to his boss, a thickset man with a wide jowly face and black hair, and greeted him with a squeeze of his fleshy hand.

Severinov prepared a fresh pot of coffee while they waited for TENOR. The American arrived soon afterward, calm but businesslike and keen to press on quickly. He took the coffee that Severinov offered and sat in a green armchair, facing Severinov and Rostov on the sofa opposite.

After some brief inconsequential chat about ongoing transport difficulties around Islamabad, Rostov opened the proceedings. "What do you have for me, my friend?" he asked.

TENOR leaned back on the sofa and sipped his coffee. "You realize there is little time left to maximize the benefits this relationship offers, don't you?"

Rostov nodded. "Gorbachev seems determined to pull out, if there's agreement with your White House and President Zia. It looks likely that might happen in the next few weeks."

"Yes. So, let me give you this." TENOR took a piece of paper from his pocket and handed it over.

Rostov scanned down the sheet, holding it so that Severinov, sitting next to him, could also see. There was a list of seven mujahideen warlords, six of whom Severinov recognized, and next to each name was a location and an inventory of what had been recently supplied by the ISI.

The last name on the list was the only one Severinov had not seen before: Javed Hasrat. It had the name of a village next to it: Wazrar, Khost-Gardez.

Severinov sat motionless for a few seconds. The village name was burned firmly into his head. He had signed off on a helicopter gunship attack on it only a few weeks earlier as part of Operation Magistral after receiving some vague intelligence that a muj Stinger gang was based there.

But then, immediately after the attack, the mujahideen had shot down two of his Hinds, killing one crew instantly and massacring the survivors in the second chopper in gruesome fashion.

It had left him determined to wreak revenge, if he could

only find out who was responsible. It was even more important to him than career progression. Now Severinov realized that TENOR might have that information.

"I've never heard of this Javed Hasrat, but he looks like a serious threat," Severinov said, consciously keeping his voice level and matter-of-fact. He read the inventory next to the name. "Twenty Stingers. My God, the ISI must have some confidence in him."

He knew that each Stinger cost about $70,000, so entrusting a single mujahideen with almost $1.5 million worth of lethal hardware seemed like a massive, even foolhardy, leap of faith.

"Does the CIA keep records of all the Stingers issued to the ISI?" Rostov asked.

"Yes, but there's no records of what happens to them after that. Once they hand them over, that's it. They have no idea where the ISI is dispatching them."

"So how do you know where these have gone, then?" Rostov asked.

"You don't need to know that," TENOR said. "Just believe me when I tell you those numbers and names are accurate."

TENOR leaned forward and looked at Severinov. "You're looking puzzled?"

"No, not puzzled," Severinov said. "Just intrigued. The mujahideen shot down two of our Hinds at Wazrar last month using Stingers. I'm just wondering if it was this Javed Hasrat who did it." He jabbed his finger on the name listed on the sheet of paper.

"Quite possibly," TENOR said. "I doubt the ISI is handing out Stingers to more than one muj in the same area."

Rostov glanced at Severinov. "Can you get that checked out, whether Hasrat was involved?"

Severinov nodded, and Rostov turned back to TENOR.

"How much longer are the Stingers going to keep coming, though? That's the question?" He drained the remains of his coffee.

"Not long," TENOR said. "If your country withdraws, that'll be it, I'm guessing. Head office is already worried about what's going to happen to all the weapons out there. What will the muj do with them? They're very worried they'll get sold on to terrorists—the Iranians, Hezbollah, you name it."

"I'm sure you're correct," Rostov said. "So what are they going to do?"

"The CIA is already tasked with trying to come up with a much more detailed inventory than that one," TENOR said, pointing at the sheet Rostov was holding. "If I can get hold of a copy, that should give you an even better idea of which muj commanders have what weapons. I think that will then form the basis for a CIA strategy to buy back the weapons—probably at a price much higher than they cost in the first place. Maybe double. Washington is going to be happy to pay the price if it means avoiding Stingers getting in the wrong hands."

"Hmm. Interesting," Rostov said. "Do you know who's handling this investigation?"

"A CIA officer. Joe Johnson," TENOR said.

Rostov leaned back on the sofa, clasping his hands behind his head. "There might just be an opportunity in this—if we can get some of these Stingers off the mujahideen. We could arrange a concentrated spate of nighttime raids by two Spetsnaz I have close links with who will work utterly confidentially for me. There would be no paper records of the operation, no documentation—all secret. The payback on such raids could be enormous."

Severinov grinned inwardly—he had been thinking exactly the same thing. He didn't like his boss, whom he found difficult and prickly to work with, but he had to admit, Rostov never missed a trick, especially when it came to matters of financial gain, and he had taken Severinov into his confidence at an early stage in their working relationship. It could be a mutually profitable relationship.

TENOR gave a sliver of a smile and nodded. "Yes. There's definitely money to be made. But it'll only work if Johnson's project fails. If he compiles an accurate list of where the Stingers have gone, it won't."

"Why?" Rostov asked.

"Because there will then be too much suspicion if a large number of them suddenly appear from some other unexpected source not on the list when the repurchase scheme begins. Langley will ask too many questions."

Severinov nodded and leaned forward, glancing at Rostov. "I understand," he said. "This guy Johnson's project does need to fail. I will think about a solution."

CHAPTER FIVE

Tuesday, February 16, 1988
Islamabad

Joe Johnson checked his watch and glanced at the driver of his maroon Honda Accord. He had been going for two hours now on a convoluted route around the ordered streets of Islamabad and the far more chaotic ones of neighboring Rawalpindi.

Most of the time he had been in the car, but he had also spent time on foot among the crowds outside the teeming Rawalpindi railway station. Then he mingled with office workers heading into the Islamabad business district, where he bought food from a street seller and walked alongside students and diplomatic staff. Afterward, he rejoined his car at the end of an alleyway.

He had taken his time over his surveillance detection route because of the high risk of being tracked by the ISI, but now all his instincts told him he was black. There was no sign of coverage.

He instructed Fawaz, the driver, to turn right off Constitution Avenue along Main Margalla Road eastward toward Quaid-i-Azam University, and then gave further directions as they drew closer to the location for his meeting with MILLPOND.

Fawaz turned on his windshield wipers. It was a typical chilly February day, and the drizzle was becoming heavier. Two youngsters on Vespa scooters hooted as they buzzed past, cutting in dangerously close to the Honda to avoid a truck coming in the opposite direction.

Within ten minutes, Fawaz had pulled up outside an anonymous three-story concrete apartment building among a cluster of identical properties less than a kilometer from the university campus.

Johnson zipped his jacket, got out, and made his way to the front door of the building. The dust lying thick on the ground had turned to a sludge in the drizzle.

He unlocked the door to the communal area, climbed the stairs to the second floor, and let himself into the CIA-owned apartment, one of several safe houses used by the Agency for meetings with sources from within government, academia, and the security and intelligence services.

Johnson had wasted no time in arranging the meeting with Haroon, with whom he had already built a good rapport. He was anxious to find out exactly what progress the agent had been making in building relationships with the mujahideen and hoped he could make use of whatever information was being picked up.

He also knew Haroon was taking significant risks. President Zia and the director-general of the ISI, General Hamid Gul, had long banned ISI officers from socializing with CIA officers, even at diplomatic functions. And given the Pakistani ban on Americans meeting with Afghan rebels, or even crossing the border from Pakistan into

Afghanistan, being found out would mean an instant prison sentence.

Yet Gul's ISI staff were underpaid, and the lure of $800 a month in cash was a massive incentive for someone on a Pakistani government salary. Clearly Haroon, who had two children he needed to fund through university, thought the rewards worth the risk.

After ten minutes, he arrived. A thin, academic-looking man, forty-two years old, with a narrow mustache and black hair slicked back over his scalp, Haroon had already spent two decades with the ISI.

Johnson opened the conversation in Pashto, as he normally tried to do out of courtesy. He had picked up the language rapidly and was becoming fluent, adding to the Russian and the German he had learned in Berlin and the Spanish from high school and Boston University.

Quickly, however, Haroon switched to his accented English. "Joe, I have only a half hour, so we need to work quickly," he said as Johnson served him a cup of black tea. He straightened his neatly ironed blue cotton shirt and picked up the cup.

Johnson explained what he wanted. First, better connections with mujahideen commanders to help him to understand where the weapons supplied by the CIA were going. Secondly, the need to somehow capture a Russian Hind and a communications van.

"That's a challenge—a Hind and a comms van," Haroon said, raising his eyebrows.

"I know. But it's an order from on high," Johnson said. "It has to be done, somehow."

"Right now, your best chance of getting the Hind, and probably the van, is in the Khost-Gardez Pass," Haroon said. "The Russians are showing signs of retreat but are still carrying out some operations. There is a commander I know there who might be able to help, a man called Javed Hasrat. He is well connected and has had some success using your Stingers to shoot down Hinds. If he thought you might be able to supply him with more Stingers, he might be cooperative."

"Perhaps you can arrange a meeting," Johnson said. "And how do you know about the Hinds?"

"A meeting may be possible," Haroon said. "And the information about the Hinds came from some excellent connections I have built in the KHAD. They know everything."

Johnson nodded. His regard for Haroon had just risen a notch or two. The KHAD—Khadamat-e Etala'at e Dawlati—was the Afghanistan intelligence agency, but in reality it was simply the local arm of the KGB, who controlled it with an iron fist. If Haroon had found a route into the KHAD, then that might produce information useful not only to the CIA but also to the mujahideen.

"I'm glad you're making good progress inside the KHAD," Johnson said. "Are there any other potential recruits you're working on?"

"A few."

"Such as?" Johnson asked, although not expecting Haroon to give anything away.

"Oh, I am hopeful about some. Just one example, the head of the KHAD and KGB archives in Kabul, the keeper of the secrets, as I call him. He is in charge of all the KGB files. A man named Abdul Akbari."

"An Afghan is running the KGB archives?" Johnson asked, slightly surprised.

"He is one of the most senior, most trusted KHAD men. He has been for training in Moscow at the Lubyanka. He is KGB in everything but name."

"Well, good luck with him," Johnson said. "Have you had any meetings yet?"

"One so far. I'm organizing another. If I can get him, he will be a useful source of information for you."

"*Useful?* I'm guessing he'd be outstanding," Johnson said. "Keep me informed about your progress. The other thing that would be extremely helpful would be any names and locations of senior 40th Army commanders or KGB officers," Johnson continued. "Particularly any of those who have been involved in operations against the mujahideen, including bombing villages."

"I understand," Haroon said. "You want to either recruit them or kill them. So, you only have one of two things in common with the mujahideen—they also want to kill the Russians, but recruiting is not a possibility." He laughed at his own attempt at a joke.

Johnson shrugged. "Personally I'd prefer to recruit them, but sometimes we don't have an option." Like Jameson, he wouldn't be doing any killing himself, that was for sure. The muj would do that job far more efficiently, sometimes facilitated by MI6.

"This Javed Hasrat," Johnson said. "Can you try to get him into one of the towns or cities just over the border for a meeting?"

Haroon leaned back in his chair and sipped his tea. "I'll talk to him. But I do not think he will take the risk of going into a populated area. You will almost certainly have to go up to his village or some other location in the mountains if you want to see him."

"The mountains?" Johnson said. "The Khost-Gardez, you mean?"

Haroon gave a thin smile. "Yes, Joe. The Khost-Gardez Pass. I will see if I can arrange it."

"I think that's going to be too much of a risk, going there," Johnson said.

Haroon shrugged. "Take it or leave it. It's the only way

you will see him. He will not venture into a town, I assure you."

Johnson tried to remain impassive. But the thought of a trip to the Khost-Gardez to meet a heavily armed mujahideen commander in winter was not an appealing one, especially as it was right in the middle of a zone being targeted by Russian gunship helicopters and ground forces. Why the hell couldn't he meet somewhere sensible?

"Tell him no," Johnson said. "I'll need to meet him somewhere less isolated."

CHAPTER SIX

Johnson still had the remnants of a hangover when he arrived at the CIA station.

He liked a beer and more than the occasional vodka or scotch, and as a result had found his first weeks in the intensely Muslim environment of Pakistan to be tough. Outside of official embassy functions it was illegal to drink alcohol, which the Pakistanis put in the same bracket as hard drugs.

But he had quickly found there were ways around the legal constraints. At a cocktail party for expat businessmen at the US embassy, Johnson had befriended an American food importer, Dennis Clarke, who had a house not far from the embassy with a basement in which there was a private bar, well stocked with a variety of whiskies, and even a small dance floor.

Dennis, a former US Army Special Forces operative with

previous links to the CIA, had switched his career path to the more lucrative private sector. He proved a useful source of local information and contacts for Johnson, who in turn passed on helpful security updates. When Dennis had invited Johnson around for a few drinks on the Tuesday evening, Johnson took full advantage. The two of them made serious inroads into a bottle of eighteen-year-old Dalmore. Afterward, Dennis told him he could use the basement bar anytime if he needed to entertain someone.

Johnson had the offer firmly tucked away at the back of his mind when he joined the CIA team of three, including Alec Jameson, for the MI6 meeting that Watson had instructed him to join.

The meeting was always held in a secure, soundproofed room with a high-security steel door that had been specially built within the CIA station—it was a room within a room.

When the usual delegation, also of three people, arrived from the MI6 station at the neighboring British embassy, Johnson was pleasantly surprised to see someone he had noticed from the diplomatic circuit but whom he hadn't yet had a chance to speak to beyond a cursory introduction.

Jayne Robinson was a slim, tanned woman with short dark hair and a white smile who had arrived from London a few months earlier.

As the meeting progressed, Johnson realized that there was a crossover between his role and Jayne's. He would need to build better links with the muj, and despite the major difficulties that women had operating in Afghanistan, she had already made two covert trips to the Khost-Gardez Pass area herself in the previous month, together with male colleagues. They had built links with two mujahideen leaders, although not Javed Hasrat.

Later, the two of them had a brief discussion about the need to meet separately, where they could discuss in greater detail about how they could combine their resources. They agreed to regroup later that afternoon and exchanged phone numbers, both for their offices and their apartments.

Johnson also quickly realized that not only was she quite attractive, but also she had a typically dry British sense of humor that he felt drawn to.

So far, Johnson had found Islamabad to be a social back-water. But maybe things were looking up. He decided to call Jayne later and invite her to Dennis's house for a drink and a chat about the Khost-Gardez situation.

* * *

"Have you had this room swept recently?" Johnson asked Dennis. The thought that one of the intelligence services operating in the Pakistani capital, most likely the ISI, might have planted bugs or other surveillance equipment in any property used by Westerners was never far from his mind.

Johnson glanced around the basement bar, which was painted a dark shade of maroon. Ornate mirrors and water-colors of women in a variety of suggestive poses were placed around the walls.

"Yes, two weeks ago," Dennis replied. "I had a private company in to do it. They found nothing. Don't worry." He waved his arm toward the small bar in the corner of his base-ment. "There you are, it's all yours."

Johnson glanced at Jayne, who was scrutinizing the three black leather sofas and an armchair that encircled a long, low wooden table. In the corner, colored lights were rotating and flicking specks of blue, green, red, and yellow over a small dance floor.

"I'll put some music on," Dennis said. "I've got a great soul compilation. You'll like it." He walked to a stereo system behind the bar and flicked a switch on the cassette deck. A

Luther Vandross track, "Never Too Much," started playing through concealed speakers.

"I need to go to a meeting over dinner," Dennis said. "You can stay as long as you like. My housekeeper is on the top floor. When you're ready to go, just ring the bell on the bar there and she'll let you out." He nodded and made his way toward the stairs.

Jayne smiled. "This is good," she said. "I think I'll start with a vodka and lime. With ice."

Johnson mixed her drink and fixed himself a Jack Daniels. When Johnson had called her at home earlier that evening, after getting back to his apartment from the embassy, she hadn't hesitated in accepting his invitation for drinks.

One hour, a couple more drinks, and a wide discussion around Pakistani and Afghanistan politics later, he had established that their agendas were quite similar.

Both had been partly inspired by the opportunity to help the US in its fight against communism as the Cold War continued. They had grabbed at the opportunity to go to Afghanistan after realizing the extent to which the Russians had carried out a virtual genocide across swathes of the country during their occupation, beginning in 1979.

Operationally, both were interested in forming links with several of the same mujahideen leaders—including Javed Hasrat—with a particular focus on trying to disrupt Russian control over the Khost-Gardez Pass. Johnson gave her only a vague outline of the likely time frame for implementing any plans the Agency might have to develop such links, and Jayne was similarly vague.

His initial impression that Jayne was not only good-looking but also very professional and smart continued to deepen.

Aged twenty-six and from Nottingham, she had been at MI6 for more than three years, having completed a degree in international politics at Cambridge University, she told him. She, like Johnson, had quickly picked up Pashto to add to her other languages, including Russian and Spanish. Johnson was impressed.

The tape finished, so Johnson put on the second volume of the soul compilation, poured two more large drinks, and sat down again.

"Strange that we Americans have to turn to you straight-laced Brits to get the dirty jobs done," Johnson said.

"What do you mean, the 'dirty jobs'?"

"Acquiring guns with silencers. Who'd have thought it?"

"We've got our uses," Jayne said. "And actually, we've been at this much longer than you in this part of the world. We're not so straightlaced."

"Only joking," Johnson said, smiling. "You seem anything but."

Jayne downed the remains of her drink in one gulp. "We'll need to bloody well look out for each other over the next few months," she said, fixing her gaze on Johnson.

"You may be more right than you know," he said.

Then she stood, wobbling slightly. "Come on. We've talked enough. Shall we dance?"

Johnson shrugged. "Okay."

He followed her to the small dance floor in the corner and, taking her lead, soon found a good rhythm. It had been a while since he'd been to a club or disco, but he did enjoy dancing, particularly after he'd had a couple of drinks and lost some of his inhibitions.

Now, dancing alone with Jayne, the alcohol definitely helped. Otherwise he would have felt self-conscious with just the two of them, especially as he hardly knew her.

A couple of tracks later, on came a much slower, smoother Lionel Richie number, "Stuck on You." Jayne moved a little closer and a couple of times, her hand briefly touched Johnson's as she danced, her rhythm now much slower.

Was she making a move on him? The alcohol made it difficult to think clearly, although at the back of his mind, Johnson couldn't help feeling undecided about whether it would be a good thing. He certainly felt attracted to her physically, but he was well aware that starting a relationship, no matter how casual, with an intelligence officer from another service would be far from sensible.

His indecision meant that for a minute or two, he did nothing. But then, Jayne placed her hands on Johnson's shoulders and pulled him closer, now moving in a slow, languorous manner.

She was fairly tall, probably five feet nine, athletic, and had shed a loose-fitting top to reveal a tight cotton T-shirt beneath. Given that her jeans were also showing a hint of her curves, Johnson couldn't help suddenly feeling a little aroused. From the look in her eye, he was guessing she might be feeling the same. Or was that just wishful thinking?

He placed a hand on each of her hips, swaying in time to the music as he did so. In response, she clasped her hands behind his neck and pulled tighter again, so her breasts occasionally lightly touched his chest.

Johnson started to feel a little light-headed as his adrenaline flowed, mixing with the alcohol he had consumed.

But then, as the track ended, she leaned back, smiling at him, and slowly squeezed his shoulders before stepping away. "That was fun," she said. "So nice to have a drink and a dance. It's been a long time—not since I was in London."

"Yes, great," Johnson said. The next track began, a faster dance number. "Shall we keep on dancing or do you want to have another drink?"

Jayne shrugged and glanced at her watch. "Umm, I'm not

sure," she said. "It's getting late. Do you think we should get going? We don't want to overstay our welcome here."

She walked slowly back to her seat. Johnson, feeling slightly confused, followed. Maybe she too had the same doubtful thoughts running through her head about the wisdom of starting something between them.

He considered the idea of asking her back to his apartment for a coffee, but then decided that, as he had known her for just a short time, it might not be the best idea.

"Perhaps you're right," he said. "We shouldn't stay too late. I'll turn the music off."

Maybe it was just wishful thinking, he thought to himself.

CHAPTER SEVEN

Friday, February 19, 1988
Islamabad

Unusually, Johnson's second meeting of the week with Haroon was at the same safe house near Quaid-i-Azam University that he had used previously. Normally he rotated locations for meetings with his agents, but this time he had no choice, as the others were in use.

He took extra care with his surveillance detection route to ensure that there was no ISI stooge on his tail.

Haroon was half an hour late and explained that he too had been taking additional precautions and had been forced to do a couple of additional loops around the city after suspecting that one of the ISI's surveillance team had been tailing him. It had turned out that the man had simply been on his way for a haircut.

"Joe, I have a lot more than you to lose if things go wrong," Haroon said, stroking his mustache.

"You don't need to tell me that," Johnson said.

Haroon, who seemed more on edge than at the meeting earlier in the week, took out a pack of cigarettes and offered one to Johnson, who accepted. Haroon lit both the smokes with a brass lighter, then came straight to the point.

"I have spoken to Javed again," he said. "He wants to meet you, and he said there was something you need to know about in connection with a senior American person who has been involved in some sort of under-the-table deal to supply arms to certain mujahideen commanders."

Johnson stiffened. If an American had been lining his pockets by supplying muj with weapons, it definitely wasn't part of any official project that the station currently had ongoing.

In fact, it could threaten the whole CIA strategy to arm the mujahideen, which had been planned carefully to avoid giving the Russians any concrete proof of American involvement that they could parade on international TV.

"He told you about an American supplying the muj?" Johnson asked. "Who the hell is that? Based in Pakistan or somewhere else?"

"He did not say and would not tell me. I do not think he quite trusts me. He said that would be something he may discuss with you depending on how your meeting goes, but he might not. He was vague."

Johnson's immediate private thought was that this might simply be bullshit and part of a setup designed to draw him into a meeting. His second was that some of the ISI top brass were probably privately doing exactly the same thing as this unknown American—including, for all he knew, Haroon.

"Do you think this information is true?" Johnson asked.

"Quite likely. I have no reason to think it is not true."

"And is he agreeing to meet?"

"Yes, Joe, but he will not meet you in Jalalabad or one of the other towns, like I told you before. He wants you to go to his village. He is quite insistent."

Johnson took a deep drag on his cigarette. "Well . . . shit."

CHAPTER EIGHT

Friday, February 19, 1988
Kabul

Severinov glanced at his watch. It was one o'clock. He opened his battered old leather briefcase and removed a gray electronic box the size of a large reference book, comprising three rectangular modules joined together and with various dials and knobs on the top.

He laid the unit on the table in front of him and checked that the modules were properly connected.

Severinov had acquired the Strizh high-frequency burst radio transmitter and receiver the previous year and had wasted no time in deploying similar units to the small group of agents he had managed to recruit among the mujahideen. They used the radios to keep him informed about planned attacks on Soviet bases and troop units and about the location of weapons, most of which had clearly been supplied by the Americans, despite their efforts to disguise the source.

Given the lack of other communications links across

Afghanistan, the radios were vital to allowing Severinov and his KGB colleagues to coordinate their plans. The units allowed encrypted messages to be transmitted at very high speeds, taking just a second or two and thus minimizing the risk of interception.

After checking the battery, Severinov flicked a switch, and a small red rectangular liquid crystal display on the top of the unit came to life. He glanced out the open window of his apartment, on the top floor of the four-story Makroyan block built by the Soviets for their administrators, embassy staff, and other workers.

The gray concrete block, with its modular style and metal windows, had been deliberately chosen by Severinov. The reason lay not in its aesthetics but solely because it faced south in the direction of the segment of the Hindu Kush mountains that separated Kabul—itself well over a mile above sea level—from Gardez and Khost.

Severinov carefully aligned the radio unit until he was able to get line of sight to a radio repeater in the barren khaki-colored mountains.

Next, Severinov turned a dial on the receiver module on the left side of the unit. For the next few minutes, he paced up and down the room of the KGB safe house, waiting.

He had asked his mujahideen contact, Sandjar Hassani, code-named GOATHERD, to obtain the identities of the men responsible for shooting down and killing the crews of two Mi-24s outside Wazrar at the beginning of January.

If there were no incoming messages, it probably meant that Sandjar had been unable to find an opportunity to sneak away to transmit from the cave outside Wazrar that he used to store his equipment.

Severinov lit a cigarette and propped his elbows on the window ledge, gazing out beyond the Makroyan complex to the street beyond. A string of yellow-and-white Kabul taxis threaded their way at a snail's pace up the street, negotiating a path through a jumble of market stalls selling kebabs, watermelons, and grapes and dodging past pedestrians, trucks, and assorted animals. A small boy kicked a chicken, which ran away, squawking. A posse of relaxed-looking Russian 40th Army soldiers stood talking and laughing on the corner of the street, AK-47s strung across their shoulders.

After spending the last two of his thirty-one years in Kabul, Severinov had gotten used to the chaos, the dust, and the poverty. He had even begun to grow fond of the place and its lack of regimentation, compared with his previous posting in the KGB's busy Berlin *rezidentura* or with life in Moscow. Both Rostov and Severinov were based in Kabul, but Severinov spent more time in Islamabad and other parts of the region than his boss. He enjoyed the travel; such trips were primarily to meet with the KGB officers and agents whom he managed, and the role had given him a new feeling of freedom, one that he had never known growing up in Moscow.

His mother, Olga Orlov, as she was known before her marriage, had also worked for Stalin, although she never spoke of the Soviet leader. She was a cook at his Kuntsevo dacha outside Moscow from 1944 until 1952.

She met Sergo during that period, and the couple married in 1950. Seven years later Yuri was born. They remained in the Russian capital, where Severinov later studied for a degree in economics at Moscow State University prior to joining the KGB in 1980.

Severinov finished his cigarette and put the stub in the bin. Then, at five past one, the unit behind him beeped quietly. He walked to it and read a message that was scrolling across the red LED display in Pashto.

KGP 1305 GOATHERDX. NOW HAVE CERTAIN

ID ON LOCAL GROUP RESPONSIBLE FOR
MI24 SHOOTING DOWN AND KILLING OF
CREW IN KG PASS JANUARY 2X WILL SEND
SECOND MESSAGE WITH IDX ENDSX

Three minutes later the unit beeped again and another
message arrived. Severinov's stomach flipped over as he read
what it said.

KGP 1308 GOATHERDX. THE KGP GROUP
LEADER AND STINGER OPERATOR IS JAVED
HASRAT. HELPER IS BAZ BABARX ENDSX

Severinov stood looking out the window for several
minutes. The detail from Sandjar, corroborating the name
Javed Hasrat that he had picked up from TENOR, meant
that he now had work to do.

* * *

Severinov pushed down on the accelerator of his cream-
colored Lada and overtook a truck as he headed southwest
along the road bordering the filthy brown waters of the Kabul
River to his left. He swerved slightly to avoid a group of
giggling girl students who were crossing the road, all dressed
in Western clothing. In contrast to the rural towns and
villages, he saw very few of the more educated women around
Kabul wearing burkas or veils—usually only the poorer ones
who shopped in the markets.

Severinov was well used to the forty-minute journey from
his apartment to the KGB's offices, near the headquarters of
the KHAD, at Dar-ul-Aman, in south Kabul.

He drove past the zoo and turned left down the long Dar-
ul-Aman Road. Right at the far end of the road was Dar-ul-

Aman Palace, where most of the important government and military buildings were located.

But he didn't need to drive that far. The KGB offices were around halfway along the road, near the Russian embassy in the Allauddin area. Security in the whole area was tighter now than it had been prior to a mortar attack by mujahideen guerrillas on the KHAD's offices a couple of years earlier.

Severinov flashed his pass at the gate, parked the Lada, and made his way past the security post at the front gate of the building, bristling with unsmiling 40th Army soldiers. He continued up to the fourth floor of the building, where his office was located just down the corridor from his boss.

The KHAD was supposedly elevated in status since its former head, Mohammad Najibullah, had been appointed president of Afghanistan by the Soviets the previous year. But everyone knew the KHAD was now just a puppet on a string for the KGB, which controlled almost all its activities. Indeed, the so-called KGB advisers to the KHAD, based in Severinov's offices, were actually its directors.

Severinov knocked on the dark brown varnished door marked with Rostov's name on a cardboard nameplate and waited until his boss's sonorous voice summoned him in.

"I've just had confirmation from Hassani that it was Javed Hasrat at the K-G Pass who shot down those two Mi-24s in January," Severinov said, making his way to a wooden chair in front of Rostov's desk. He sat down and unbuttoned his coat.

"Good work," said Rostov. "There's definitely a double opportunity here. If we can kill Hasrat, we will get considerable credit in Moscow, as it should free up the pass for more chopper patrols. And if we can acquire Hasrat's remaining stock of Stingers at the same time, we could feed them back into the CIA's repurchase program. That could be big money."

"My thinking exactly," Severinov said.

"I'm going to set you this challenge," Rostov said. "I want you to bring Hasrat in for a little questioning."

Severinov raised an eyebrow. "You want him brought in here? Not killed?"

"If we apply a little persuasion, Hasrat may give us leads to other *dukhi* commanders who also have Stingers. It could be a case of one brings two, or even three or four."

The Soviets all called mujahideen *dukhi*, the Russian word for "ghosts."

Severinov nodded. Prior to taking his current role, Rostov had done a stint with the KGB's counterintelligence and security division, Line KR, during which he had spent six months working in the basement of the Lubyanka. There he learned every trick in the book on how to extract information from unwilling prisoners. He had then passed on much of his knowledge to Severinov, who had soaked it all up.

It supplemented the knowledge Severinov had acquired from his father, who apart from being Stalin's close bodyguard was also an enforcer who was expert in interrogation. His usual tools included a rubber truncheon and a spring-loaded steel rod, used to systematically break his victims' leg and arm bones.

Rostov's idea of persuasion would probably involve ordering him, Severinov, to take Hasrat down into the basement of the KHAD building, where there was a special room equipped with most of the devices imaginable—and a few that weren't.

Severinov had seen men half skinned alive down there as the final stage in a process that had earlier involved beatings with a baseball bat. The wooden bat was one of Rostov's prized possessions, confiscated from a CIA spy who had been thrown out of Russia back to his homeland. Electric shocks using crocodile clips attached to genitalia and cigarette burns were also part of the usual routine.

"That sounds like a good plan. You can leave it to me," Severinov said. He leaned back in his chair, his mind already beginning to switch into another gear to address the potential issues involved in plotting an operation deep into muj territory in the K-G Pass.

"Good," Rostov said. "You will need to start a KHAD file on Javed. See Abdul."

Severinov frowned. "Yes, I'll get it done."

He never relished his dealings with the notoriously prickly Abdul Akbari, head of the archives at the KHAD. The archives, in another part of the basement away from the interrogation rooms, carried detailed records of every operation and individual whom the KHAD and KGB had contact with.

But there was one other issue that needed resolving. "Leonid, comrade," Severinov said. "If this operation is going to pay off, we will also need to decide what to do about the CIA officer, Johnson, whom TENOR mentioned. If he finds out which muj commanders have which weapons, and the Americans realize some of Hasrat's Stingers are missing, it will be difficult to get the compensation on offer when our intermediaries funnel them back into the buyback program."

"Yes," Rostov said. "He's a complication." The KGB chief leaned back in his chair. "I want you to dispose of Johnson. He may cross the border into Afghanistan, which Pakistan has ordered the Americans not to do. So wait until he's in Afghanistan and hit him. Then there's less chance of the Pakistanis making a fuss about it."

PART TWO

CHAPTER NINE

Monday, February 22, 1988
Islamabad

Watson leaned forward and propped his chin in his right hand, elbow fixed on the table, his gray-blue eyes locked onto Johnson's. There was silence for at least fifteen seconds.

Johnson folded his arms and waited. It was one of Watson's usual intimidatory techniques. Next would come the critical jab, normally laced with a dose of sarcasm. He was right.

"So, it's fine to screw about for a while? There's no rush, is there?" Watson said eventually. "Doesn't really matter if the Appropriations Committee slashes the Afghanistan budget and we're out of a job, does it?"

Johnson sighed inwardly. "All I'm saying is, going to some mountain village in the K-G Pass, over the border when we're not meant to, and right in the likely line of fire of trigger-happy gunship helicopter crews is something we might want to think carefully about."

Is the stupid bastard deliberately trying to put me at risk?

Alec Jameson, sitting next to Watson, shook his head. "We'll do a risk assessment, but when it comes down to it, in this situation, we've no choice. It comes with the territory, buddy. You know that."

Johnson had just finished briefing Watson and Jameson on his discussions with MILLPOND about Javed Hasrat. Vic, who was also attending the meeting, gently kicked Johnson's ankle twice under the table as a warning not to say anything inflammatory toward his boss.

"Listen," Watson said. "It's vital we meet Hasrat. So go for the initial meeting in the K-G to show goodwill. These guys need to know we're prepared to give them respect and meet them more than halfway. Then insist on the follow-up meeting being where it suits us. Okay?"

Watson eyeballed Johnson again. There was clearly no room for negotiation here.

"I'll get it fixed," Johnson said.

Watson looked at his watch and stood. "I've got a meeting to go to," he said. He nodded at Johnson and Vic and walked out of the room, leaving them with Jameson.

Johnson watched Watson depart. It was hardly surprising his boss's wife, Carol, had refused to move to Islamabad with him. She had stayed at home in Virginia, not far from Langley, with their six-year-old daughter. Life was doubtless a lot more peaceful at home with Watson away for lengthy periods. Nobody in the CIA station seemed to hold out a lot of hope for their marriage.

"Is there anything else we need to cover?" Jameson asked.

"I can't think of anything," Johnson said. He stood to leave, as did Vic, and opened the door of the meeting room.

Johnson was about to step outside when Jameson called after him. "One other thing. That MI6 officer on their liaison team who was in our meeting the other day, Jayne something."

Johnson felt a slight jolt go through him.

"What about her?"

Jameson inclined his head to the side. "Just go carefully. Working together doesn't mean you have to get close outside work."

How the hell?

"We liaise closely in a working sense and that's it," Johnson said. He could feel his voice cracking a little. "We need to. Why?"

"Right. Good," Jameson said. "You know what I'm saying."

Johnson, taken completely by surprise, could only nod. "Is this something you've discussed with Robert?" Johnson asked.

Jameson shook his head. "There's no need to if you're sensible." He indicated with his hand that he should leave.

On the way back to their workstations, Johnson and Vic passed Watson's office. Standing outside, next to Watson's secretary, Pauline Stark, was a tall Western man with muscular shoulders, wearing a dark suit and carrying a briefcase. He passed a business card to Pauline, which she placed on her desk.

"Joe, there's a letter for you," Pauline called out. She picked up an envelope and held it out.

Johnson walked to her desk and took it. As he did so, he caught a glimpse of the logo on the man's business card, which was lying the wrong way around. Kay Associates, it said. He couldn't see a name.

"Thanks, Pauline," Johnson said. He rejoined Vic and the two men continued down the corridor.

"Coffee?" Vic asked.

"Yeah. Let's go," Johnson said. "I need to get out of this place. We'll ask Neal if he wants to go too." He inclined his head back toward the man outside Watson's office. "Do you know who that is? I saw his business card. Kay Associates."

"Nope, never heard of it or seen him before."

"Me neither. I'll see if I can get Pauline to tell me another time."

Half an hour later, after a three-mile drive through the well-ordered streets of Islamabad to Kohsar Market, Johnson, Vic, and Neal settled down at Espresso, one of several coffee shops they visited at random. There, in a well-positioned corner table with a clear view of the rest of the café and the doors, the three men finally felt safe to chat without the risk of surveillance.

"First," said Johnson, "how the hell did Jameson know about Jayne Robinson? I've met her once outside work and that was after I did a long SDR. I'm certain I wasn't followed."

Vic shrugged. He looked around the coffee shop, which like most of the outlets at Kohsar Market was used mainly by wealthy Pakistanis and foreign diplomats. "Someone tipped them off, maybe. Dennis Clarke?"

"Doubt it," Johnson said. "He's got no reason to do that. I'm a lot more useful to Dennis than Watson is, so why would he?"

He went on to brief Vic about Javed's comments, passed on by MILLPOND, about a high-level American delivering unofficial supplies of weapons to mujahideen commanders.

Vic almost spilled his coffee as he sat bolt upright. "An American supplying Stingers? Shit. Well, there's more than a few in the arms business operating internationally."

Neal, who had moved to Islamabad from Langley at around the same time as Johnson, also looked shocked. "Maybe those stories about McDonnell are true, the money-grubbing bastard," he said.

Seb McDonnell was the US ambassador to Pakistan, an

apparent workaholic whose favorite topic of conversation was money, investments, and the next buck.

Johnson shook his head. "No, I can't see it. We all know he's a bastard to work for, but he's way too much of a career guy. He'd never risk doing anything like that." He inclined his head. "Jameson?"

"Possible, but I doubt it," Vic said. "He's also a greasy pole climber, just like Watson. It's certainly not me, that's for sure. There may be other candidates, but I don't know who."

"I was never suggesting it was you, you idiot," Johnson said. "But it might be worth doing a bit of surveillance on McDonnell, just to check him out."

Vic chuckled and pushed his metal-rimmed glasses up his nose. "Yeah, I like the idea of putting someone on our own ambassador. But who would we get to do the job?"

"Got to be a Pakistani," Neal said.

Johnson nodded. "Haroon knows a couple of recently retired ISI guys who he says are good on the street. We could hire them. Dirt cheap."

Vic nodded and took out a pack of cigarettes, offered one to Johnson, who accepted, and then lit them both with a match.

"We may get to the bottom of it if we can arrange this meeting with Hasrat," Johnson said, drawing heavily on his cigarette. "I'm going to have to meet him anyway if I'm going to make any headway with the Hind and the comms van."

Vic grimaced. "Hmm. All I can say is, good luck with that. Try not to involve me."

CHAPTER TEN

After working all morning in his office on the fourth floor of the KGB's offices in the Dar-ul-Aman area, Severinov finished his notes on Javed Hasrat, inserted them into a thick brown paper envelope, and headed down the worn wooden staircase.

After leaving the building, he glanced left along Dar-ul-Aman Road to the palace, a splendid turreted European-style stone mansion atop a small hill that dominated the surrounding area. After being restored following fire damage, it now housed the Ministry of Defense.

From there, he walked around the corner and entered the KHAD offices, also built from local stone. After clearing security, he descended to the basement, walked along the corridor past the gray steel entrance to the detention rooms, and entered the archives department through a set of ancient wooden double swing doors.

It took his eyes several seconds to become accustomed to

the gloom. But there behind his desk as usual, sat the chief archivist, Abdul Akbari, a tall, wiry man with an unkempt black beard and a pair of black-rimmed glasses.

Behind Akbari, stretching deep into the basement, was an array of shelving that rose from the floor to the high ceiling and housed files on tens of thousands of Afghans from all walks of life. The files formed the basis of the KGB's and KHAD's daily decisions on who to arrest, torture, and sometimes kill.

Severinov approached the desk and forced a smile. "Greetings," he said. "I've got a new file for you."

Akbari, an Afghan who Severinov guessed was in his thirties, fixed him with a gimlet-eyed stare that lasted several seconds. Eventually he nodded and held out his hand, into which Severinov placed the file on Javed Hasrat. He hated dealing with Akbari, who seemed to dislike not just him but all his Russian colleagues too, despite the status he had acquired with senior KGB officers in Moscow, who seemed to trust him completely—doubtless because of the quality of information he provided.

The Afghan pushed his glasses up his nose and scrutinized the filing notes that Severinov had written in precise handwriting on the front of the folder.

"Thank you," Akbari said. He looked at Severinov over the top of his glasses with an unblinking gaze, his face muscles motionless. "Anything else?"

"Only one thing. Do you have a file on a Joseph Johnson, a CIA officer based in Islamabad, who has interests in Afghanistan?"

Akbari pursed his lips. "CIA? I don't recall that name, but I'll check." He shuffled off to a set of gray filing cabinets and opened a drawer. Severinov watched as he began rifling through an array of index cards.

Two minutes later he returned, shaking his head. "Strangely, no. You said he's based at the Islamabad station?"

"Yes."

"How long has he been in Islamabad?"

"Not sure."

"We will need a file on him. Can you start one for me?"

Severinov nodded. "I'll drop it in here for you later in the week."

* * *

Monday, February 22, 1988
  Islamabad

After arriving back at his third-floor apartment on the corner of Hill Street and Street 12 in Block F-6 of the neighborhoods that formed Pakistan's capital, Johnson felt like pouring himself a whiskey. It was past six o'clock in the evening, and after managing to acquire a couple of bottles he had gotten into the habit of relaxing with a glass after finishing work. But this time he resisted the temptation; he needed to think, not drink.

He was well aware that he was entering into dangerous waters by planning a foray over the border into Afghanistan against the direct orders of Pakistan's powerful ISI, which was in turn operating on the instructions of President Zia.

But risk was part of the work, as Jameson had said, and if Watson was instructing him to do a specific job, he would have to do it. His train of thinking reminded him that he was a couple of days overdue in carrying out his weekly sweep of the apartment to check for any listening devices or cameras.

The ISI were notorious for planting such equipment, and on the assumption that all cleaning and domestic workers were quite likely to be on the ISI payroll, all staff based at the US embassy were strongly advised to carry out regular checks of their accommodation, even those lucky enough—unlike Johnson—to have secured an apartment within the walled grounds of the embassy. His apartment block was three and a half miles away to the northwest.

Then came a loud beep from the buzzer phone unit mounted on the wall next to the door of his apartment. It was the security guard, calling from the downstairs lobby.

Johnson picked up the phone. "Yes?"

"Sir, I have a lady to see you here."

"A lady? Who is it?"

"She says her name is Jayne Robinson. I have checked her ID."

Johnson hesitated, feeling simultaneously slightly elated and confused. Why was Jayne visiting his apartment? They hadn't spoken since the fairly abrupt end to their alcohol-fueled dance at Dennis Clarke's house the previous Wednesday evening, and he was certain he had only given her the phone number of his apartment, not the address.

"Send her up, please."

He opened the door of the apartment and looked out along the corridor in the direction of the stairs. A couple of minutes later, Jayne appeared through the fire door, wearing a pair of loose-fitting slacks, a brown jacket, and a headscarf.

She stood there momentarily, then continued along the corridor to where Johnson was waiting.

"Don't worry," she said before he could open his mouth. "No tail."

He nodded. "Okay, good. You'd better come in."

But Jayne shook her head and beckoned Johnson out into the corridor.

She leaned in close toward him and whispered. "I did a routine check of my apartment this morning and found a bug behind an air vent. A small thing: high-sensitivity, battery-powered transmitter. Voice activated."

Johnson's eyes widened a fraction. "Shit. It's got to be ISI or KGB."

"Maybe. We're getting it analyzed, but our technical guys said it's not a piece of kit that either of them normally uses," Jayne said. "It's worrying because the only people who come in there are the cleaners, at least as far as I know."

"Any idea how long it was there?"

"It could only have been since last Tuesday at the earliest, because I swept the place on Monday evening myself and it was clean."

"You checked the vent?" Johnson asked.

"Yes, of course."

Johnson glanced back toward his apartment door. "I was only just thinking I should check over my place. Best do it now before we talk."

"I'll give you a hand."

Johnson nodded. "Thanks. Then if it looks clear, I'll get a technical guy in from the embassy next week to do a full sweep. I'll begin with the living room, if you can start in the kitchen?"

"Sure."

They moved silently into the apartment, where he pointed Jayne toward the small kitchen. A few seconds later he heard her moving items in his dish cupboard.

Johnson walked into his living room. He usually started with the light fittings and electrical sockets. He removed a small set of screwdrivers from a drawer, turned off all the electrical circuits apart from the main ceiling lights, and set to work. First, he unscrewed the front plates from all the power sockets and checked the cavities behind. There was nothing there. He moved to the two bedrooms and carried out a similar procedure, followed by the kitchen, pausing only for a few moments to watch Jayne, who was checking all the tins and packets in his food cupboard.

Johnson unscrewed and checked all the light switches. Again nothing, so he moved on to the light fittings. Again, he found nothing.

Johnson then went through the utility closet in the hallway, but he drew a blank. Above it was a cupboard that housed the electric meter. He stood on a chair and switched on a flashlight and looked inside. The meter was mounted on a board, which in turn was screwed to the wall.

Johnson stared at the meter. On a whim, he decided to unscrew the board that held the meter, something he had watched the embassy's technical expert do on his last visit. He took a larger screwdriver and loosened the four big screws that held it until the board began to lean forward away from the wall.

Gradually, Johnson loosened the screws farther until he could see behind the board, where there was a cavity in the brickwork through which a thick power cable emerged and connected with the back of the meter.

He shone the flashlight into the cavity and then jerked back a little. He whistled softly to attract Jayne's attention, and she immediately emerged from the kitchen, her eyebrows raised questioningly.

Johnson put his finger to his lips, indicating to her to keep silent, and picked up his find: it was a small black box, around the size of two cigarette packs, that had been lying behind the meter. A rigid wire, about eight inches long, protruded from the back, pointing at forty-five degrees into the air.

Johnson unclipped the back cover and removed the battery to disable the device before speaking.

"Sonofabitch. Look at this," he whispered.

"Same as in my apartment," she said.

"Why doesn't that surprise me? There might be more. I'm calling the technical guys."

He called a special hotline to the technical team leader at the embassy and, aware that his phone might also be bugged, used a code word to signal that his apartment had been compromised and that an urgent visit was required.

Forty minutes later, after he and Jayne finished their own silent search and found nothing, one of the embassy's team turned up—the same technician who had swept Johnson's flat previously. He spent an hour with a range of electronic detection devices checking the apartment while Johnson and Jayne sat on the sofa, watching.

The man had almost completed his search when his detector suddenly emitted a loud beep as he ran it over a plant pot on a table in the hallway. He threw Johnson a glance, picked up the pot, and tipped the soil and plant into the garbage can.

Lying at the bottom of the pot was another device, half the size of the first one, that also had a wire aerial. The technician removed a battery from it and placed the device carefully into a bag.

"I think that's it," the tech said eventually. "I'm confident the rest of your place is clear."

After he had gone, Johnson finally relaxed. He made a pot of coffee, and he and Jayne sat on the sofa in his living room.

He wondered if he should mention their dance at Dennis's house, but Jayne immediately launched into a work-related conversation, not giving him the chance.

"I was thinking about what we were discussing the other night," she said. "You know, about cooperating on our cross-border interests, and I said that we'd need to look out for each other in the coming months—"

"Bloody well look out for each other, you said," Johnson interrupted.

She laughed. "Did I? Yes, I probably did. And I meant it. I guess I've just done that."

"Yes," Johnson said, glancing at the empty plant pot that was lying on the floor. "You might need to do some more. It seems I'll be going to the K-G Pass sooner than I indicated."

"Well, I can give you a briefing based on my two visits. Is this to see Hasrat?"

"That's the plan."

Looking at Jayne, Johnson felt an immediate surge of optimism inside him. She was definitely attractive and smart. Back home, he would have followed up on their previous encounter. He didn't have a girlfriend, and although he often seemed to have Kathy on his mind, he had long ago put her in the category of a friend he had liked a lot during their time at Boston University but with whom nothing had ever happened —even though all their friends said it should have.

Anyway, Kathy, who had majored in English literature, was working for a magazine publisher in DC now, and he was in Islamabad, a million miles away.

He tried to focus on work matters as a way of diverting himself from the attraction he felt for Jayne. He talked her through the concerns he had about the risks involved in a cross-border operation and the time pressures he was now under, given the demands of senators on the Appropriations Committee in DC. Those demands, in turn, were being passed down the line by the CIA leadership.

"Watson's been quite aggressive about the operation," Johnson said. "Too much so, in my view. Yes, we need to do something, but safety should still be a priority."

He paused and studied Jayne. "And Jameson has been on my case about you."

"What do you mean?"

Johnson shrugged. "He warned me not to get too close to you outside work. The subtext was that he thought we were."

"Shit. What the hell?" Jayne's voice rose, and she folded her arms. "Did he know about the drinks at Dennis's place, then?"

"Possibly." A thought flitted across Johnson's mind. "I'm just thinking. Whoever put the bug in my apartment, or yours, might have heard our phone conversation when we arranged to meet at Dennis's place."

"Yes, it's quite possible. My phone is in my living room, just a few yards from where the device was, yes."

Johnson stared at the ceiling, trying to recall what they had discussed on the phone that evening.

"I don't think we discussed anything too sensitive," Johnson said. "But—do you think it's possible, if someone knew we were going to meet at Dennis's, that they might have bugged his house as well before we got there?"

"Not that we talked about anything in great detail," Jayne said, "although we did mention Hasrat and the K-G Pass."

"Yes," Johnson said. "And the fact that it was just the two of us down there in an apparently cozy one-to-one meeting that nobody else was told about might be enough for my boss."

"You'd better bloody well get Dennis to get his basement swept, then," Jayne said.

"Indeed," Johnson said, his mouth set in a thin line. "I will."

CHAPTER ELEVEN

Tuesday, February 23, 1988
Sulaiman Mountains

Javed and Baz scrambled carefully down the narrow stony path, skirted around a boulder the size of a two-story house, and stood behind a bush. There they waited for several minutes, carefully scrutinizing the scene in the treeless ravine below them.

It had taken three hours of travel by mule to reach the camp, where they had arranged to have a short meeting with the mujahideen commander who dominated the region around Khost, Jalaluddin Haqqani. He was long established as a dangerous opponent of the Russian occupying army. Javed knew that Haqqani was already plotting to retake the city of Khost from the Russians.

After Javed's contact in the ISI had approached them with a proposal for a meeting with a CIA officer, Joe Johnson, Javed and Baz had decided, after a long discussion, to go ahead. But they also wanted to run the idea past Haqqani.

Neither of them wanted to get on the wrong side of a man who, if upset, could easily destroy them.

The meeting place had been agreed upon with one of Haqqani's aides. But Javed now wanted to ensure that he wasn't about to walk into some sort of trap.

Everything looked in order. The camp was constructed beneath a lip of brown stone that protruded several meters from an almost vertical cliff face, and the cave behind it was perfect for hiding the small gathering from aerial scrutiny by Russian helicopters or cameras operating from satellites.

"Come, let's go," Javed said. The two men made their way down the path toward a flat area of ground between the camp and a small stream that flowed away to their left.

Immediately, they were spotted by armed guards. One of them shouted to them in Pashto to stop and wait. He approached and asked a series of questions until he was satisfied they were who they claimed to be. After thoroughly searching them and their mules for hidden explosives, he led them into the cave.

There, sitting on the ground with two other men, was Haqqani, an imposing man with a long, straggly beard whom Javed had met several times before but still did not feel that he knew well at all. Haqqani, like most of his Pashtun colleagues, was dressed in a thick khaki camouflage jacket that looked as though it had come from US Army surplus. Haqqani was well known for his links with the CIA, who were thought to have channeled large amounts of dollars in his direction. Most of the other men in the camp wore a gray *shalwar kameez* and either a black turban or a *chitrali* cap.

However, Haqqani was wearing an off-white turban with thin red stripes that looked incongruous with the jacket. He stood and welcomed Javed with a traditional Pashtun greeting in his usual reserved manner.

"Salaam alaikum," Haqqani said. *Peace be upon you.*

"Walaikum salaam," Javed replied.

Normally, Javed would have expected to be offered a range of food and drink during such a visit, but Haqqani apologized and said that his supply arrangements had been affected by a Russian helicopter attack the previous day, and his men were now all hungry.

"I am sorry, but we only have that," he said, indicating toward a bowl on the floor that contained pieces of flat bread. They all sat and Javed and Baz both took a piece.

Haqqani wasted no time in getting straight to business. "I understand you want to have a meeting with a CIA officer. Why?" he asked.

This was predictable. It was entirely possible that Haqqani already had a relationship with this CIA officer and didn't want anyone else encroaching on his territory. But when Javed gave Johnson's name, the mujahideen commander shook his head. No, he didn't know this man.

"I understand this American wants to discuss the capture of an Mi-24 helicopter and a communications van," Javed said. "This could enable us to earn cash that could be used to purchase weapons and ammunition. It may also allow us to source more weapons from the Americans that may be useful against the Russian infidels. More Stingers."

"More Stingers would be useful," Haqqani said, smiling.

Javed went on to mention the killing of his wife and youngest daughter in a Russian helicopter attack on his village.

Haqqani nodded. "Yes, I have heard about what happened in your village. You need to avenge it." He looked gravely at Javed. "You have my permission to go ahead with your meeting. Just do not let the personal aspect cloud your judgment. Take what you can from the Americans and use it against the Russians—but the American Johnson too is an infidel. So do not get too involved. You might need to kill him as well one day."

Javed nodded. "Of course."

"When are you planning this meeting, and who else in your group knows about it?" Haqqani asked.

Javed hesitated, glancing at Baz. "I don't know when yet. I still need to confirm all that. And we're the only two who know it's happening. I don't want to take any risks."

* * *

Thursday, February 25, 1988
Kabul

Severinov leaned over the red LED display on his Strizh burst radio positioned on the window ledge of his office in the KGB building and read the message closely. His strategy of carefully cultivating sources in all camps was now really starting to pay dividends.

He had been waiting for a message from Sandjar Hassani in the K-G Pass with some detail about Javed Hasrat's plans to meet his CIA or ISI handlers. But there had been nothing. That source appeared to have run temporarily dry in recent days. Severinov hoped his agent hadn't been compromised.

Instead, the information was coming from another direction. This message, from TENOR, now offered him a great opportunity to deal a huge blow to the mujahideen in the K-G Pass and to the CIA in one hit.

KAB1 FROM ISL4TENX CIA JOHNSON MEET
WITH HASRAT PLAN FRI FEB 26 C.8PMX
LOCATION HANI VILLAGE NEAR KHOSTX
NO INTEL ON EXACT ADDRESSX ENDX

Severinov gazed out the window and across the southern suburbs of Kabul to the raised splendor of the Dar-ul-Aman Palace in the distance, bathed in sunlight against the backdrop of the dark mountains behind.

He walked to his desk, sat down, and picked up his secure phone, then dialed a number for Colonel Vitaly Pavlov, commander of the 50th Aviation Regiment, who ran the fleets of Mi-24 gunship helicopters in Afghanistan.

CHAPTER TWELVE

Friday, February 26, 1988
Sidgi, northern Pakistan

The Land Cruiser slowed as it came into Sidgi village. Johnson pulled his black turban back into position and straightened the *shalwar kameez* in which he was dressed. Since learning he would have to operate across the Afghanistan border, he had let his beard grow and had applied theatrical makeup to darken his skin. It had worked surprisingly well. He doubted he was going to convince any Afghan up close for more than a couple of seconds, but at a distance, he should be able to pass for a Pashtun.

Over to Johnson's right, a lone camel padded along a small field, pulling a plough that was being steered by a farmer, who hobbled behind it, almost bent double. The field, and the one next to it, were the only visible patches of green in an other-wise brown, barren landscape.

To his left, a flat-roofed shop constructed of rough stone

had freshly slaughtered goats and sheep hanging on hooks outside. That must have been the local butcher.

Operation Espresso was well underway—Vic had given it the tag in the name of their favorite Kohsar Market hangout, after rather obliquely making the linguistic connection between *Javed*, *java*, and *coffee*.

After starting at six o'clock in the morning on a nine-hour journey from Islamabad with two men from the CIA's operations support team—Phil and Simon—Johnson was feeling more than a little tired and tense by the time they arrived at Sidgi, near the border with Afghanistan.

Haroon had finally managed to negotiate a compromise meeting location. Rather than rendezvousing in the K-G Pass, which would have been nightmarish to reach, Javed Hasrat had agreed to meet near the village of Hani, fourteen miles south of Khost. It was much more easily accessible from Pakistani territory but still technically under Russian control.

The only issue now was getting there and back safely. The CIA crew, both of whom were ex–Special Forces, had picked up two guides that Haroon had supplied en route. There was Toryal, a black-bearded Pashtun with a barrel chest, and Wali, a slight man with metal-rimmed glasses. Both promised that security would not be a problem. But Johnson was by now accustomed to his Pakistani hosts occasionally overpromising and underdelivering.

Both guides sat next to Johnson in the rear of the Land Cruiser. Phil, who was driving, accelerated as he reached the northern end of Sidgi. Now driving under directions from Toryal, he pushed on toward the Afghanistan border, about three miles farther up the dirt road, which was punctuated with potholes and mini ravines where rainwater and melted snow had drained off.

At the end of the road there was a T junction, where next

to a telegraph pole that lurched at an angle stood a pale-faced man holding four mules by the reins. Toryal told Phil to stop and raised a hand to the man as the vehicle braked to a halt.

Toryal turned to Johnson. "There is no road on the other side of the border, so from here, we go by mule for three kilometers over the hills until we join the road to Hani." He indicated with his hand toward a steep array of clay-colored hills that rose ahead of them. "Don't worry, it is all under control. It is safe. When we reach the road, we will continue by another vehicle. I have a contact from near Khost who will meet us."

"Right," Johnson said. "I hope it is safe."

Before leaving Islamabad, Johnson had given a detailed briefing to Watson and Jameson about his plans for the rendezvous and then, as a precaution, had shared a similar briefing with Jayne because of her knowledge of the area and MI6's strong links with the ISI.

But although Phil and Simon were going to remain in the area until the operation was complete, they were not exfiltration experts. If things went wrong, Johnson would rely rather on Jameson and Jayne putting plans into action to get him out. But both seemed a long distance away, and the only means Johnson had of contacting them was via his portable battery-powered burst radio, which he carried in a small backpack and which would allow him to transmit and receive short messages if necessary. He also carried a Global Positioning System tracker device in the bag.

Johnson eased himself out of the Land Cruiser, agreed with Phil and Simon that he would meet them at the same drop-off point later that night, and followed Toryal to the man with the mules, who were all standing motionless.

Toryal introduced the man as Spin. "Not his real name. It means 'white,'" he said. "Because of his face." Johnson nodded. The man definitely had much paler skin than the others.

"Have you ridden one of these before?" Toryal asked.

"Horses a few times," Johnson said. "I don't really know what I'm doing." Spin gave a thin smile but said nothing.

But ten minutes later, Johnson was astride one of the mules, as were Toryal, Wali, and Spin. A dog barked behind them and the mule suddenly jumped a little, throwing Johnson off balance. He grabbed the reins, wobbled, and only just managed to stay in his saddle. The other men laughed.

"Okay, we need to go now," Wali said, suddenly serious. "We don't have a lot of time."

He jerked on the reins, shouted something unintelligible to the mule, and set off at a steady walk along the track heading north into the hills. Toryal followed, and Johnson, trying to recall his teenage horse-riding lessons back in Portland, tugged on the reins and did likewise. Spin brought up the rear as they rode in single file at a sedate pace.

Thankfully for Johnson, the mule did not repeat its initial skittishness and moved steadily with minimal guidance behind the others as they climbed an increasingly steep and stony path into Afghanistan.

By now, it was quarter past five; the sun had set, and dusk was well advanced. Ahead of them, to the north, the snow-covered higher slopes of the Hindu Kush mountains were visible, rising sharply into the blue-black of the evening sky. The only sounds were the clicking of the mules' hooves on the stony ground and the animals' occasional heavy breathing.

After twenty minutes, they crossed a ridge and began descending again, down a tortuous zigzag path that reduced the mules to a crawl. They rounded a rocky outcrop, and there, waiting at the end of a dirt road, was a vintage green Land Rover, covered in dents and dust.

Spin walked to a rock at the side of the track, lifted it with one hand, and took a key from underneath. Smiling briefly at Toryal, he unlocked the vehicle and indicated to the others to climb in.

Toryal turned to Johnson. "This is it. Welcome to Afghanistan, my friend. Seventeen kilometers to Hani. There we will find Javed Hasrat, if Allah is willing."

* * *

Friday, February 26, 1988
Hani, eastern Afghanistan

The silhouette of the Hindu Kush mountains rose high into the sky, which was growing blacker by the minute as the remaining scraps of daylight dissolved. Spin piloted the growly Land Rover along the single-lane dirt road seemingly by feel because he had left his headlights off, and the vehicle bumped and jolted over assorted larger rocks along the way, occasionally throwing Johnson sideways.

The track was dusty and dry, and it clearly hadn't rained for some time.

At last, the outline of a few flat-roofed, mud-brick houses appeared through the gloom, gradually growing denser in number as the Land Rover headed into the village. A flock of sheep standing in the middle of the road scattered as they approached, and a man in a bulky turban and a long beard was silhouetted against a doorway by candles burning in the room behind him.

A group of children, each probably no more than six years old, ran around a corner, shrieking. Upon seeing the Land Rover they stopped, now silent, and stood watching intently as it passed.

Spin braked to a halt at a crossroads, then turned sharply left along a dirt road that curved around behind some more houses. Johnson saw a tall stone wall to their right that was more than double head height. It looked incongruously well built compared with the others they had passed.

The Land Rover came to a halt outside an emerald green gate in the wall, covered with gaudy pictures of flowers and plants that appeared to have been painted by children.

The gates swung slowly open, and Spin drove into a small yard at the rear of the house, his lights still off.

"This is where we are meeting Javed," Toryal said.

Spin turned the vehicle around so it was pointing back toward the gate again. "Just in case we need a quick getaway," he said, pulling up the hand brake.

Johnson picked up his backpack containing the burst radio and climbed out of the Land Rover along with the others as a tall man with a white beard, a white *chitrali* cap, and a patrician air about him padded up to them, a Kalashnikov strung casually across his shoulder.

Toryal greeted the man deferentially and turned to Johnson. "This is Yousuf Khan; he's the village chief. It's his house," he said.

Johnson exchanged greetings with Yousuf and shook his hand. He knew who Yousuf was from his pre-mission briefings: he had been responsible for bringing a lot of US-sourced weapons, including Stingers, over the border into Afghanistan to use against the Russians. The village chief used camels and mules to distribute the weaponry to other mujahideen bases in the mountains.

Toryal spoke quietly with Yousuf, then turned to Johnson. "Javed Hasrat is inside the house, waiting for you," he said. "Come this way, we have only a little time." He turned and led the way through the open door and into a long room lit by two paraffin lamps.

There were three men sitting cross-legged on the floor on a long, colorful cloth. In front of them was a low wooden table laden with dishes of yogurt and rice, lamb, chicken, flat bread, and other food. They all stood when Johnson and Toryal entered, and one of the men stepped forward.

Square-shouldered and with a long beard, he fixed Johnson with a pair of eyes that glinted black.

"This is Javed Hasrat," Toryal said.

Johnson held out his hand to Javed. "Salaam alaikum," he said.

"Walaikum salaam," Javed replied, shaking Johnson's hand. "We can speak English. I know it."

"Thank you," Johnson said. "You speak it better than my Pashto."

Javed gave a short laugh and glanced up at Johnson's turban. "I like the disguise. Very good. Sit and eat; then you can explain what you want from us, and I can explain what I need from you."

"Thank you," Johnson said. "I just need to send a quick message to my people first."

He took out his burst radio, turned it on, and tapped out a one-line missive.

JJ99 TO C5 AND M11X LOCATION A WITH
TARGETX WILL CONFIRM ON ENDINGX
ENDSX

When he had finished, he pressed transmit. A red LED light glowed for a couple of seconds, indicating that the transmission had been successful, and then a green light replaced it, indicating the unit had connected with the receiver—an electronic handshake, as the CIA's technical team called it.

The message, which went to the CIA station in Islamabad and Jayne Robinson, was a prearranged signal to ensure they knew where he was and that the operation was going according to plan. He turned the radio off and put it back into his bag, which he zipped shut.

As they ate, Johnson ran through the need to have more clarity over where CIA-sourced weapons were going if the supply was to continue, the strategic importance of capturing a Hind and a comms van, and the requirement to make sure there was no letup in the mujahideen battle to drive the Soviets out of Afghanistan.

"The US doesn't want Gorbachev saying on TV in Moscow that Russia is pulling out while on the ground it's a very different story," Johnson said. "The two need to be aligned. It would be a good step toward that if your people can recapture Khost."

"Yes, I agree," Javed said.

"What reserves of weapons do you have? Enough Stingers, RPGs, and so on, which I imagine are the most useful in your territory?"

Javed hesitated and looked at Johnson through narrowed eyes. "We only have five Stingers left. Supplies of those from the ISI have dried up—we could quite easily use up all five in just one engagement. And there are only a couple of RPGs. So if you are able to get some for us, it would be very useful."

"Okay, we will see what is possible."

"You will need to move quickly," Javed said. He twirled his index finger around in a series of rapid circles in front of him. It was an unusual gesture, Johnson thought. "And your request for a Hind and a comms van. You realize what a big demand that is and how difficult it will be to achieve?"

Johnson nodded. "Yes, I do. And that's why we're prepared to offer a large amount of money as a reward, a bonus, if you're able to obtain them for us. We can offer fifty thousand dollars for one of them, intact and with minimal damage." Actually, the Agency was prepared to go to

$100,000 for either, but Johnson decided not to reveal his full hand.

There was a sharp intake of breath not just from Javed but some of the others in the room. He scrutinized Johnson for a few seconds. "*Fifty thousand* dollars?" Javed said. "Is that your word, your promise?"

"It is my word," Johnson said, with as much finality in his tone as he could. "In cash."

"There is something else I would need too," Javed said. He looked around the room and gestured toward the door as he said something in quick-fire Pashto that Johnson didn't completely understand. Everyone began filing out of the door to the yard outside.

When the room had emptied, Javed lowered his voice to a whisper and spoke again. "The money is good, but in return for obtaining either a Hind or a comms van, what I also want is this: a US passport for myself and my two daughters, permanent visas for all of us, and air tickets to New York."

Johnson was taken aback. "Why do you want to move to the United States?"

Javed gestured with both hands. "You have seen what life is like here. The Russians have killed my wife and youngest daughter, and they will do the same to me and my other two daughters if they can. There is no future for my children in this country."

"They killed your wife and daughter?" Johnson asked.

He then sat in silence while Javed briefly described how his village had been destroyed by Hinds the previous month.

"I hear what you are asking," Johnson said, when Javed had finished. "I will discuss it with my superiors when I return to Islamabad. What is your job, outside the mujahideen, I mean?"

"I am in the energy industry. I work for the state electricity utility, DABM, in engineering and planning."

"Those are useful skills. It should help with your visa," Johnson said.

He knew that now was the time to press his host on the issue of the CIA arms supply source. "Actually, while we are alone, I have a question of my own to ask. I understand from our mutual friend that you may have some information about supplies of weapons to some mujahideen commanders from a source within the CIA, operating independently of our colleagues in the ISI. I would be interested to know who that might be."

"That is something we could discuss, yes, and I might have some information that—"

Suddenly Javed stopped talking and looked up, as if listening carefully. Johnson strained to hear what Javed was concentrating on, and there it was: the distant but distinct clattering sound of multiple helicopter engines coming from the northeast, getting rapidly louder outside.

Two of Javed's men rushed into the room and began jabbering at high speed in Pashto.

Javed jumped straight to his feet, an alarmed look on his face. "We need to get outside now," he said to Johnson, his voice rising. "Russian helicopters."

CHAPTER THIRTEEN

Friday, February 26, 1988
Islamabad

Jayne was halfway through a plate of chicken stew in her MI6 accommodation inside the British embassy compound when the burst transmitter receiver on the window ledge beeped softly.

She swore under her breath. It was the second message in less than forty minutes. The first, letting her know that Johnson had gotten to his destination, was a relief. Surely Joe couldn't have finished his meeting that quickly, she wondered.

Still chewing a mouthful of food, she got up, walked to the unit, and carefully read the message on the small red LED display.

JJ99 TO C5 AND M11X URGENTX UNDER
RUSSIAN CHOPPER ATTACKX BEGIN EXFILX
ENDSX

"Shit, shit," Jayne said out loud. "How the hell . . . ?"

She checked the frequency on which the burst message had been sent and wrote it down on a pad. 483.996 MHz. Then she tapped in an immediate reply.

MII TO JJ99 AND C5X RECEIVED UNDERSTOOD WILL DOX ENDSX

Then she pressed send and waited for the red and green lights to indicate a connection.

Jayne was convinced that Operation Espresso had been kept watertight. Only the very small number of people on the joint CIA and MI6 team and a handful of support personnel knew anything about it. Unless the Russians, by some huge coincidence, had decided to launch a gunship attack on the tiny village of Hani just at the very moment when Johnson and Javed were there, it was evident a mole had been at work.

Jayne grabbed the secure phone on a table next to her living room door and punched in a number for her station chief, Mick Avery.

"Mick," she said after running as quickly as possible through her security password process, "Operation Espresso is blown. I've just had an urgent message from Joe to me and Alec saying there's a Soviet gunship attack on the village, and he's requesting us to implement the exfil."

"Well, he's obviously alive," Avery said, his voice level and calm. Too calm. Jayne always had a suspicion that he took beta blockers. "Is the attack finished? Was it just a routine blitz to scare the horses?" he asked.

"I don't bloody know," Jayne said. "It was just a short burst message. No update as yet. But we will need to mobilize the Pak helicopter unit out of Miran Shah immediately. I can get on to ISI right now if you can give me clearance to do that."

"You'll need to call Jameson first," Avery said.

"For God's sake, yes, of course." *Why does process always rule with these guys?*

"Right. Get on with it," Avery said. "I'll get off the line now. Good luck."

Jayne hung up. Miran Shah was a Pakistani air base with a seven-thousand-foot runway only seventeen miles from the Afghanistan border and twenty miles from Hani village, where she now imagined Johnson was scrambling for safety—and for his life.

There were five heavily armed French-built Aérospatiale Puma helicopters based at Miran Shah, along with an array of other military aircraft. Four of them were operated by the Pakistan Air Force, but the fifth was run by the United States, having been flown in from Peshawar to provide backup for CIA operations in the region.

In theory, the US Puma was barred from any cross-border work into Afghanistan, and its movements were meant to be monitored rigidly by Pakistani military radar, quite apart from the Afghanistan and Russian radar units that everyone assumed were also watching all aircraft movements in the northwest of Pakistan.

In practice, the Puma's highly skilled crew carried out more than the occasional operation cross-border, usually flying at low altitudes to avoid radar. It also had a black anti-infrared coating painted on the outside of its fuselage to help avoid detection during nighttime operations.

Johnson, Jameson, and Jayne had put the Puma's operational team on standby for Operation Espresso as a precaution. Now it was starting to look like a sensible insurance policy, Jayne thought.

Before she could call Jameson, he rang on her secure phone.

"Jayne, I'm assuming you've picked up the message from Joe," Jameson said.

"I was about to call you. Yes, I have," Jayne said, her voice rising in pitch. "I'd like to know how this thing leaked to the Russians, assuming it's not just a coincidence. But let's sort that out later. I can coordinate things at this end. I've spent time up in the Khost area and know it reasonably well. I also know the helicopter crew at Miran Shah from a previous operation."

That was stretching the truth a little. She, along with two male colleagues, had flown in with the crew to Miran Shah once for a meeting with a local tribal chief, but that was the extent of it.

However, she had an urge to take personal responsibility for this operation.

Ever since the evening when she had danced with Johnson at Dennis Clarke's house nine days earlier, she had felt a strong affinity with him. At times, she had even regretted not following their dancing through to a physical conclusion. But she had never felt comfortable beginning physical relationships with men she didn't know well. And professionally, she felt it would have been foolish to have started something so quickly, given that they would be working closely together.

Now she felt determined to do what she could to extricate Johnson from what was almost certainly a potentially deadly situation.

"Fine," Jameson said. "I'm happy for you to do that. You need to get on to the chopper crew immediately."

Jayne felt a twinge of annoyance at Jameson telling her something that was blindingly obvious. "Of course. I'll call them now. Will update you later." She hung up.

Five minutes later, she was completing her call to the Puma crew leader and pilot, Captain Franz Alperstein, who promised to get his aircraft airborne immediately. Due to the

sensitivity of the highly classified CIA cross-border operation, she did not give the name of the case officer she was
asking them to pull out.

"Don't worry," Alperstein said. "Your man has a GPS
transmitter on him, right?"

"Yes, correct," Jayne said.

"Fine. Our kit should be able to get us within twenty
yards of that. We'll have him out of there."

* * *

Friday, February 26, 1988
Hani, Afghanistan

The deafening sound of helicopter engines no more than a
few hundred yards away was all Johnson could initially hear as
he ran from the door to the Land Rover. He had just climbed
in when the rumble of machine gun fire began. Johnson
counted two Russian Hinds that were now starting to strafe
the village.

"Get in," Toryal shouted as he scrambled through the
open rear door of the Land Rover. Johnson hauled himself up,
using a handle for leverage, and threw himself onto the bench
seat next to Toryal.

"Where's Javed gone?" Johnson asked.

"He's gone the other way, with his men," Spin said from
the driver's seat. He let out the clutch with a jerk. The wheels
spun for a second on the gravel surface, then bit, and the
Land Rover moved sharply forward, its lights off.

By the light from the house Johnson could see the
silhouette of a bearded man standing next to the gate in the
yard. He was holding a long tube, frantically screwing something into its bottom. Johnson recognized it instantly as a

Stinger, doubtless supplied by his own CIA, being primed for use.

The Land Rover shot out of the gate, and Johnson, turning so he could see out of the back of the vehicle, caught a glimpse of a Hind hovering like some kind of Jurassic hornet no more than a hundred or so feet above the main street.

Flashes were visible at the front of the chopper, where automatic fire was coming from the 12.7mm Gatling guns that Johnson knew would be fitted in the gun pod. Another Hind was doing likewise, farther away on the other side of the village. Johnson expected any minute to see the chopper crew open up with their 23mm autocannon, but so far that hadn't happened.

"Do you think they're after us, or is it random?" Johnson asked.

Toryal shook his head vigorously. "I don't know." His eyes were practically popping out of his head, and he could hardly speak.

Johnson decided to take the initiative. He leaned toward Spin, who swung a hard right as he emerged from the gate. "Spin, stop the car."

Spin turned his head and braked but did not stop. "What? We need to get out of here."

"Yes, but get that guy with the Stinger, the missile, in here with us first. Quick." Johnson gestured with his hand at the bearded man behind them.

Spin glared at Johnson but brought the Land Rover to a halt on the track outside the gate. Then his expression suddenly softened, and he pushed the Land Rover's door open, jumped out, and ran back. Maybe it had dawned on him that this was not a bad idea.

The Hind's machine guns were still pounding away over toward the main street. Suddenly, there was a large explosion and a ball of flame shot into the sky. A gas canister, Johnson surmised.

After what seemed like an eternity, Spin returned with the Stinger operator and two other men who were each carrying Stinger tubes, which they placed in the back of the Land Rover. Two of the missile tubes had gripstocks already attached. The operator, who was also carrying a small backpack, jumped into the rear seat next to Toryal, who hadn't said a word, and aimed a toothy grin in Johnson's direction. "No problem. Allah is great," he said in Pashto.

Spin set off down the road at a tremendous pace. Johnson hoped that the dust presumably being thrown up behind them would not be visible in the darkness. After a quarter mile, Spin braked hard and turned left in a westerly direction away from the village and down another dirt road, still with his lights off. Now in front of them on both sides of the track Johnson could just make out boulders, larger than the Land Rover, and rock formations.

"This is the end of the track. There's cover here if we need it," Spin said. "I'm just going to stop and work out what to do next." He braked and turned the Land Rover so they could see back toward the village, about a quarter of a mile away.

No sooner had he spoken than the engine pitch of the nearest Hind rose, and the machine veered rapidly in their direction. A pair of powerful searchlights flicked on.

"Shit, now what," Johnson muttered to Toryal, who had regained some of his earlier composure.

The helicopter then turned ninety degrees and stopped near the edge of the village. Then all hell erupted. There was a series of much brighter flashes from the front of the Hind, and the unmistakable clattering sound of its autocannon rent the night sky.

"That's Yousuf's house they've just hit. I'm certain of it," Spin said. "I just hope he and Javed got out of there."

Johnson turned to the Stinger operator, then to Toryal. "Tell him to set up here. Let's take the chopper down," he said.

Toryal nodded and spoke in rapid Pashto to the man, who jumped out of the Land Rover, took his Stinger from the back of the vehicle, and began preparing it.

Johnson and the others also got out. Johnson reached inside his backpack and checked the GPS transmitter, which appeared to be functioning. The green LED on the top was flashing intermittently. It wasn't a device with which he was familiar, so he had to trust it was doing its job.

The Hind continued firing for another half a minute, then stopped and turned back in the direction of the Land Rover. The searchlights swiveled, the narrow beams of light piercing the darkness.

Then another light flicked on underneath the Hind, this time a pale pink in color.

"Goddammit," Johnson said. "Infrared. If they come this way, they'll pick up the Land Rover first—and then us. We need to get away from the vehicle and find some cover."

Johnson and the operator picked up the two Stinger tubes to which chunky gripstocks had already been attached, while Toryal and Spin carried the others. Spin led the other three men down a narrow walking path between two large boulders. Beyond them, there was a stretch of flat ground.

"Here," Spin said to the Stinger operator. "Set up here."

The operator, whose Stinger also had a sight attached, knelt down and screwed a battery coolant unit into the base of the green gripstock. Then he raised the weapon onto his shoulder, held it steady, and applied his right eye to the sight.

Johnson knew that operators were advised to wear safety glasses because of the injury risk, since the front and rear glass disks on the Stinger tube break on firing. Clearly the mujahideen didn't worry about that sort of thing.

What would the Russian pilot do next? Johnson wondered. His answer came a few seconds later when the chopper, only a quarter mile away, suddenly climbed a hundred or so feet, and its searchlight and infrared beam began scanning the patch of land where they were now hiding.

First the infrared beam then the searchlight picked out the Land Rover, bathing it in light.

"They're coming," Johnson said.

He glanced at the Stinger operator, who was preparing to fire. He had his finger pressed on the safety and actuator switch, and then Johnson heard the beep as the device locked onto the Hind. The operator pressed the uncage button and pulled back the trigger. "Allahu akhbar!" he yelled.

Two seconds later, the launch motor kicked in, sending the missile flying out of the end of the tube. But instead of forging a deadly trail across the night sky and destroying the Hind as intended, it skittered across the bushes for a couple of hundred yards and dropped to the ground. A misfire.

The operator let rip with a volley of curses in Pashto, not all of which Johnson could understand. But then he didn't need a translator to know the flight motor's failure to fire meant they were now deep in trouble.

CHAPTER FOURTEEN

Friday, February 26, 1988
Miran Shah, Pakistan

Franz Alperstein strode around the Puma, making his final checks before takeoff. The chopper was well armed now, although most of the kit had only recently been added.

The team's biggest challenge had been to remove any evidence that it was being operated by the United States, because if it was shot down in Afghanistan and seized by the Russians, the covert game of the CIA supplying the mujahideen with armaments would well and truly be up. Not to mention the row that would erupt in Islamabad with President Zia, who had ordered all mujahideen-related operations to be conducted through the ISI.

Therefore, the Puma had to carry weaponry that might plausibly be found on any Russian military helicopter. That would give the CIA complete deniability if the worst were to happen.

The Puma was equipped with a number of Soviet air force

favorites, including a Gryazev-Shipunov 23mm autocannon and 12.7mm Gatling machine guns, plus Molniya R-60 Aphid air-to-air missiles with infrared homing capacity, designed to be used in aerial dogfights with enemy aircraft at close range. It also had infrared detection equipment.

Alperstein climbed into the cockpit and glanced around at his crew, consisting of his copilot, Neil Payne, who was a veteran of the US Air Force's 1st Special Operations Wing, plus two Afghan mujahideen, Izat and Janan, who would carry out any dirty work required and added a wealth of local knowledge on the ground.

The plan was to time their takeoff, which would be carried out with all lights extinguished, to coincide with the scheduled arrival of three C-130 Hercules transport aircraft from Peshawar. This would provide noise cover and distraction if there were any undercover observers in the vicinity providing information on aircraft movements to the Soviets. It wasn't a foolproof plan by any means, but it had a decent chance of working at night and was definitely better than nothing.

Alperstein settled back in the pilot's seat, strapped himself in, and waited.

Two minutes later, just as the first C-130 had touched down, Alperstein and Payne started both engines. By the time the second Hercules was approaching, they were ready for takeoff, and as the huge military aircraft touched down and the noise outside mounted, Alperstein slipped on his night-vision goggles and eased the Puma off the ground and away to the northwest into the blackness.

After more than a year operating in the region, Alperstein knew the terrain well and had mapped out a route that he calculated would take them very close to Hani village without, he hoped, being picked up by Soviet or Afghan radar.

Flying low, at no more than 150 feet, he cruised through

three consecutive valleys heading northwest until, after about twenty-eight miles, he came to the Afghanistan border at a point where a high ridge rose up ahead of them and ran at right angles northeast toward Hani village. Hugging the ridge tight, protecting him from radar scrutiny, Alperstein piloted the Puma carefully toward the point where his GPS screen was now telling him the transmitter was located.

His biggest concern was the heavily armed Hinds, which according to Jayne's account of the SOS message were attacking the village and, he had to assume, were therefore still in the vicinity.

* * *

Friday, February 26, 1988
Hani

"We need to get farther away from the Land Rover," Johnson said. "They will search all around it. Then we're screwed."

The Russian Mi-24 gunship advanced steadily in their direction at a height of around 150 feet, creating a strong downdraft. Its searchlights remained focused directly on the vehicle.

"I will give it another go," the Stinger operator said. "I'll get him this time." He put the failed tube and gripstock on the ground and picked up the second one.

Johnson had already mentally ruled out trying again, at least from their current location. If there was another misfire and the Russian helicopter crew spotted the flash when the launch motor fired, they would have an instant target to obliterate. Getting away with it undetected once was good fortune. Risking it again seemed extremely foolish.

"No," he said, raising his voice against the noise of the

chopper. "It's too dangerous. If it misfires again and we get spotted, we are dead."

"Yes," Spin said. "I agree. He indicated behind him with his thumb. "There is a ridge that way. I think we go there. There are a lot of caves in the cliff face where the ridge drops away. They may give us cover if we can get there without the Hind crew seeing us. Quick, let's move."

Johnson nodded. It crossed his mind that if Jameson and Jayne had received and acted on his emergency burst radio message, then the best chance of a successful helicopter rescue would be if they could get out of line of sight of the Hind. Trying to get below a ridgeline therefore seemed like a sensible move.

"Yes, let's go," Johnson said. "But let's take the Stingers. We may need to have another go as a last resort if we get into real trouble." He looked at the Stinger operator, who was visibly downcast at his failure but, accepting the situation, nodded. He tucked the Stinger he was carrying under his arm, while Spin and Toryal picked up the others.

Spin turned and led the way south, away from the village, along a footpath that wound its way between rocks.

As they hurried along, they could hear from behind a raucous metallic male voice erupting from a loudspeaker on board the Hind, saying something in Pashto that Johnson could only partly understand.

"The helicopter crew is warning anyone remaining in the Land Rover to get out and give themselves up, as they are going to blow it up," Toryal said. "They have given them thirty seconds."

"Okay, keep going," Johnson said. "That's a thirty-second delay that could help us."

To the sound of the Hind engines clattering behind them, they continued in single file through the maze of rocks along a path that zigzagged steadily south. Johnson struggled to determine where the path led, but Spin seemed to have no such problems and led the way with a sure-footed stride.

Suddenly, there came a deafening bang behind them, followed almost immediately by an explosion. They turned to see an orange fireball climbing its way into the night sky about four hundred yards away.

"That's the Land Rover," Toryal said, unnecessarily. "Keep going, don't stop."

Spin continued along the path. After another couple of minutes he cut right behind a rock. Johnson, second in the line immediately behind, was taken by surprise and slightly lost his balance. As he tried to retrieve himself, his left foot caught on another small rock, and he fell sideways and backward, his backside and lower part of his back taking the brunt of the impact on some rough rocks. Something sharp dug painfully into his lower back as he landed.

Spin turned around. "Are you okay?" he asked.

"Yes, I'm okay. Sorry," Johnson said, scrambling to his feet. He pulled his pack back into position and straightened his jacket. "Let's continue."

"We're right near the edge of the ridge now," Spin said. "There's a sharp drop ahead."

They slowed to a cautious walk, and Johnson decided to check the GPS transmitter after his fall, given that he had landed on his backpack when he had fallen. He put his hand into the bag and removed the device.

The plastic panel on the front had a large crack across it, and the intermittently flashing green LED had been replaced by a steady red one. Johnson swore out loud.

He looked behind him. The Russian helicopter was moving again in their direction, its pink infrared beams sweeping the ground below.

* * *

Friday, February 26, 1988
  Hani

The GPS screen mounted on the Puma's center panel had been consistently displaying a small green dot marked on a map: it showed the location of the GPS transmitter carried by their objective.

Alperstein pushed the Puma farther along the ridge, one eye on his radar altimeter, another on his forward-looking infrared screen, also mounted on the center panel. The two devices were critical to his ability to fly at low level in the dark and told him if the chopper was getting too near to the cliff face and rocky outcrops that marked the ridge.

So far, he had managed the process in textbook fashion, remaining below the line of the top of the ridge and therefore, he assumed, out of the line of sight of Afghan and Soviet radar.

He glanced again at the GPS indicator. Then he looked more closely. "Shit, the GPS has gone off."

Neil Payne, in the copilot's seat, looked at the GPS device. "It was showing a minute ago. I checked it."

"Well, it's not now."

"We'll just have to aim for the point where we saw it last," Payne said. "Keep going. It's about another mile at most."

Alperstein nodded and continued along the ridge, neatly skirting around a large outcrop of rock that jutted out into the valley.

Then something else caught his attention.

"Neil, see that? There's a chopper hovering over there, searchlights on. And infrared too, if I'm not mistaken."

"Yeah, I see it," Payne said. "Got to be Russians. A Hind."

"And it's right where we last picked up a signal."

Because of their position below the ridgeline, the Hind

was at a slightly higher altitude than them. Alperstein hoped that given they were flying with no lights, they would be invisible to the Russian aircraft.

As he continued to stare at the Hind, he caught a glimpse of a flash a few hundred yards away from it.

"There," Alperstein said. "See that flash?"

"Yes. A machine gun or something."

"Could be. Or it could be our guy on the ground."

CHAPTER FIFTEEN

Friday, February 26, 1988
Hani

"Son of a bitch, not again," Johnson said as the Stinger missile crashed into the bushes not far in front of them.

The operator threw the tube and its attached gripstock and sight to the ground in frustration and sank to his knees, his head bowed.

There was no time to think about why both Stingers had misfired. Assuming there was a reasonable chance that the flash when the Stinger's launch motor ignited had been spotted by the Russian chopper crew, they needed to get away from their current spot as quickly as possible.

But even as Johnson spoke, the Hind's engines rose in pitch and it began to move in their direction. Worse still, Johnson could see the second Hind, which had remained over the village, was now following the first and also coming toward them.

"Quick, on the ground behind that rock, away from the

infrared," Spin shouted. He grabbed Johnson by the jacket and propelled him in the direction of a rock the size of a car to their left. "Get down."

Johnson did as he was instructed, closely followed by the others.

They were only just in time. The Hind's searchlights beamed directly toward them, casting a shadow from the rock behind which they were sheltering. Then came again the mechanical voice blasting over a loudspeaker that they had heard earlier, ordering them in Pashto to give themselves up.

"I think that's a bit of bullshit," Johnson said. "I don't think they know exactly where we are; otherwise they'd be right overhead with the Gatlings going."

The metallic recorded voice from the chopper was followed by a lengthy burst of gunfire from its machine guns, which smashed into the ground to their right and left and pinged off the rocks. Johnson ducked down even further.

"Maybe I was wrong," he muttered.

Then he jumped involuntarily backward when from behind him came the clattering sound of another helicopter engine. "My God, there's another bastard coming," Johnson said.

He turned and initially could see nothing in the blackness. Then, faintly silhouetted against the night sky, he could make out, just a couple of hundred yards away, the outline of a chopper with no lights rising like an apparition above the ridgeline.

In the next second, there was a deafening whoosh and an orange explosive flash as an air-to-air missile streaked from the blacked-out helicopter, followed by a deafening burst of orange cannon fire.

Johnson's immediate thought was that this was his end. But the missile and the cannon shells scorched straight past them in the direction of the Hind.

A second later, there was an explosion that lit up the ground and the sky around them like a neon light show, reflecting downward off the clouds and momentarily turning night into day.

It was followed by another deafening whoosh as a second missile forged across the sky from the blacked-out helicopter, which triggered another eruption.

Johnson dared to raise his head above the rock to see what had happened. Not far in front of him, the first Hind was lying on the ground, lurched at an angle, its fuselage blazing. Farther behind that, the burning carcass of the second Hind was still moving, sliding over rocks, its rotor blades slashing into the ground and throwing off showers of sparks. Eventually it came to a halt. Then came a secondary explosion from the first Hind, perhaps as a fuel tank caught fire.

As the engine noise behind him grew louder, Johnson turned again to see the blacked-out helicopter approaching. Again, there came a disembodied voice from a loudspeaker.

But to Johnson's relief, it had an American accent. "This is the United States military. Please show yourself."

PART THREE

CHAPTER SIXTEEN

Monday, February 29, 1988
Islamabad

"Of course there's a goddamn mole," Johnson said. "You don't seriously think that the Russians timed an attack on an obscure, tiny village with two gunships just at that precise moment by coincidence, do you?"

He stared across the table at Jameson, who shifted in his chair.

"Who, then?" the deputy station chief asked.

"I've no idea," Johnson said, glancing at Jayne, who was sitting next to him. "I don't even know which side it's coming from. It could be someone in Javed's unit who the Russians have recruited—like they have done in so many muj groups. Or . . . " He let his voice tail off.

"Or it could be someone in the Agency, or MI6 for that matter," Jayne said, finishing his sentence for him. Johnson nodded. It was best to get the issue out in the open.

The joint CIA-MI6 group had convened at the CIA

station in Islamabad at the earliest opportunity on the Monday after the drama in Hani to get a debrief from Johnson on exactly what had happened during the abortive meeting with Javed. The team was now well into the post-briefing debate about what could have been done better.

"One thing's for sure," Johnson said. "We only got out of there alive because Jayne was on the ball so quickly at the start and then because Captain Alperstein and his guys operated superbly. I'd say we had seconds to spare."

To fly his Puma undetected into Afghanistan airspace and to ambush two heavily armed $10 million Mi-24 gunships with his R-60 Aphids was indeed no mean achievement. Johnson was confident that Alperstein would end up with some kind of award for that. He figured the Russians must be twisting their tails in knots at the inquest over what the hell had gone wrong.

"The problem is, we got nowhere near finishing the meeting when we were rudely interrupted," Johnson said. "Do we now abort the whole operation, given the risks?"

"Not an option," Jameson said. "Not with Langley breathing down our necks and with senators breathing down the director's neck. Even if calling a halt might appear to be the logical thing to do."

Johnson knew he was right. Meyer wasn't going to, and indeed probably couldn't, let Watson and his team take a breather given the imminent meetings between skeptical senators and the Defense Appropriations Subcommittee members to discuss the huge Afghan program budget.

"We're going to have to reconvene somehow with Javed," Johnson said. "That's assuming he's still alive and didn't get shot to pieces when the Hind obliterated the house. I mentioned to him about the need to keep track of the weaponry we've been funneling to the muj groups, but we didn't get into the detail of how that might be done. And same with the idea of capturing a Hind and a comms van. No detail. Apart from that, he'll be a very useful source in the future, so we need to meet again."

Johnson wasn't going to mention the added explosive detail he also hadn't been able to clarify with Javed about some unknown American delivering backdoor supplies of Stingers to mujahideen commanders. That could wait until he had hard proof.

"Are you going to fix it up through MILLPOND again?" Jameson asked.

"I'll have to," Johnson said. "I don't have any direct contact with Javed. Not yet, anyway. Don't ask me to go to one of the villages again, though. All along I was afraid something like this might happen."

"So where, then?" Jameson asked.

"That's what we need to work out," Johnson said.

The meeting broke up, and the British contingent headed for the exit.

"The boss wants a word with you in his office in ten minutes—alone," Jameson said to Johnson.

"About this operation?"

"Yup."

Johnson ran to catch up with Jayne just before she reached the stairs. "Thanks again, Jayne. You were an absolute star the way you ran that exfil."

He meant what he said. Her speed off the mark in getting the Puma crew mobilized had been the key to him and the rest of the team coming back from Hani in one piece.

She nodded. "Least I could do."

"I'll give you a call soon. We need to meet again to plan phase two."

"Glad to see you're not waving the white flag. Yes, that would be nice. Maybe same venue as last time," she said, giving him a wink.

Slightly taken aback, Johnson raised an eyebrow. "Is that the best location?"

"Don't know, but somewhere," Jayne said. There was definitely some kind of glint in her eye, Johnson thought.

Or is there? God, I don't know.

He tried to suppress a smile. "Okay, sounds good. I'll call you. I'm not jumping the gun, though. I need to meet with MILLPOND first and get him to check if Javed's actually still alive."

CHAPTER SEVENTEEN

Monday, February 29, 1988
Islamabad

"You'll need to step on the gas with this," Watson said, his arms folded on his desk in front of him. "I've just had a call with the director this morning. He's pleased the rescue operation went the way it did, but he told me again we can't afford to backpedal. We need to deliver urgently."

"Did you brief him on exactly what happened in Hani?" Johnson asked. "Surely it's damn obvious we're pulling out all the stops on this one."

"Yes. He knows. But he's under serious political pressure."

Johnson glanced around Watson's office. On the wall behind his desk, a green Stinger tube was mounted on a plaque; it was from one of the first few Stingers that the CIA had supplied to mujahideen in Afghanistan and had been used to bring down a Hind not far from the Jalalabad air base. Watson was clearly proud of it.

On the wall on one side of the window was a framed $100

bill with a caption underneath indicating it had been the proceeds of some strange bet he'd had with an old university friend years ago. Watson liked his money—everyone knew that.

On the other side of the window was a photo of Watson on safari in Zambia, pictured holding a large rifle next to a dead rhino that he had clearly just shot. Johnson was always repulsed by the image.

"All right," Johnson said. "I'm going to be getting in touch with MILLPOND anyway. So once we know Javed is alive, I'll push for another meeting quickly and see if we can make a firm plan regarding the Hind and the van, as well as more detail on the muj weapons network."

"Good," Watson said, with a note of finality. He picked up some papers and placed them in front of him, then reached for his phone.

Johnson leaned forward. "There's another thing. I'd like to think we're busting a gut to make sure the Hani leak didn't come from someone in this building. If I'm going to meet Javed again, I can't expect Captain Alperstein to swoop in on cue a second time."

"Why, are you pointing the finger at anyone specific?" Watson asked.

"No, not yet. But I am wondering," Johnson said.

"Wondering about whom?"

"Don't know," Johnson said. "It's a tight circle of people in the loop. I'm not casting any aspersions, but what's your view of those on the team at our end?"

Johnson wasn't going to mention Jameson by name, but he had always had a feeling that Watson's deputy was not a man he could rely on in a crisis. There was that indefinable air about him of keeping one too many cards close to his chest.

Watson looked slightly affronted. "I think they're solid. I mean, including Alec," he said, returning Johnson's gaze.

"Good to hear it." It hardly seemed a ringing endorsement of Jameson's integrity.

Watson folded his arms in front of him again. "Personally, I'd say the risks of a mole are much higher on Javed's side. You don't need me to point out that a few rubles from the Russians are going to be irresistible to a mujahideen living in a dirt hut."

Johnson shrugged. "That's obvious." And it was a fair point.

"Is there anyone else we should keep a close eye on?" Watson asked.

Johnson shook his head. He couldn't think of anyone, although his mind went back to his meeting with Jayne in Dennis Clarke's basement. It was a pity that Clarke hadn't yet been able to have his basement barroom swept for any sign of bugs. The businessman had been away for several days and had not yet returned.

"Let's stop there," Watson said. "Please keep me updated on where you get to with MILLPOND. I'll need to keep the director informed."

CHAPTER EIGHTEEN

Tuesday, March 1, 1988
Islamabad

Johnson leaned against the blue railings surrounding the giant bleached skeleton of an elephant and contemplated its enormous shinbones. Then he wandered around to the front of the beast and carefully read the description and biological details on a plaque positioned beneath its tusks.

The meeting location, at the Pakistan Museum of Natural History in Islamabad's Shakarparian Park, had been Haroon's idea. The plan was for them to get black before they arrived, casually bump into each other, and then find somewhere discreet to speak. A walk in the nearby park with its undulating hills could follow, at which the real business might be conducted.

After a couple of minutes, a figure materialized to Johnson's left, seemingly immersed in the intricate yet robust structure of the elephant's metatarsal bones.

"Nature. It's quite remarkable, isn't it," Haroon said, casually glancing in Johnson's direction. "Foot bones, shins, and knees perfectly designed to bear the load placed upon them. Just as our shins and knees are just right for us, to enable us to thrive and survive."

"Yes," Johnson said. "Thriving and surviving. Something that depends so much on countering the skill and cunning of the predators around us, particularly those who fly."

"Indeed," Haroon said. "You will be pleased to know that the species with whom we are mutually acquainted was not hunted to extinction by the aerial predator in recent days. He lived."

Johnson felt most of his tension immediately drain away. Javed was safe.

An hour later, after a cup of chai at the museum's café, the two men were at the top of a hill in the park, looking out over the city below and the rising green swell of the Margalla Hills in the distance.

As they walked, Johnson passed over a brown envelope containing $800, Haroon's monthly payment from the CIA. He knew it represented a small fortune to the ISI officer.

Haroon pocketed the envelope. "Thank you."

Johnson felt confident there was no coverage from the ISI for a change—his surveillance detection route had gone well, and there had been no sign of anything that would have caused him to abort the meeting.

"So, do you have any views on who the mole at Hani might have been?" Johnson asked. "It seems to me most likely that it was someone on the muj side who has Javed's trust."

Haroon shook his head. "No, my friend, I can guarantee you that. Javed has been so worried about leaks that the only person he told, apart from me, was his partner Baz. There are others he works closely with, of course. But he kept details of the time and place extremely tight with that particular meeting. You're looking in the wrong direction for your mole, I am certain of it."

Johnson was taken aback. Haroon seemed extremely confident. And this was worrying. If not on the mujahideen side, then the implication was that the leak had come from within the operational team on the CIA or MI6 side of the fence.

"I hear what you're saying," Johnson said. "Let's put that to one side. Have you made any progress with getting names of the senior KGB personnel?"

"You already have the name Rostov," Haroon said.

Johnson nodded. "Of course. It's any others we need."

"There is another man in Line PR who I understand was responsible for the raid on Hani that nearly killed you. Yuri Severinov is the name. He reports to Rostov and has been particularly involved in planning activity in the K-G Pass area. Those are the two main people, but if I get any others, I will tell you."

"Severinov. Right." Johnson committed the name to memory. "What about another meeting with Javed? Where should we do it? I can't risk going into the villages again."

"Joe, you do not need me to tell you everywhere is risky over the border," Haroon said. "I am suggesting Jalalabad. If you are agreeable, I will try to confirm it with him."

Jalalabad was now a Soviet garrison town roughly thirty miles from the Pakistan border. The normal route there from Pakistan, via the highway through the Khyber Pass, was a nonstarter, as it was without a doubt bristling with Russian security and army checkpoints.

"How the hell would we get to Jalalabad?" Johnson asked.

"If Javed agrees, I will find a way. I have a couple of ideas."

"Hmm," Johnson said. He gazed out across Islamabad. "Can you talk me through the other options first? There must be another more straightforward way to fix up a discussion with Javed than this. Can't you get him to come to us instead?"

Haroon slowly shook his head. "He will not. I have tried. He thinks there's too many risks involved in going cross-border, and he believes you should be taking them, not him. He says he is taking enough risk already, doing what he is doing against the Soviets, without unnecessarily doubling his chances of being killed or captured. After losing his wife and one of his three daughters, he says he has his children in mind. I think there's a pride issue too. He is an Afghan, remember. I have tried to explore the alternatives with him. There are not any."

* * *

Thursday, March 3, 1988
  Kabul

Severinov lit one of his usual black Laika cigarettes and inhaled deeply. It was his third in the past half hour, and the air in his KGB office was becoming foggy with the smoke. Not for the first time he wished he had some American or French cigarettes rather than this awful Russian brand.

Then he bent back over his burst radio and fired off a message to Sandjar Hassani, who had just sent him some priceless intelligence about a weapons storage sub-depot that the ISI and the CIA had apparently jointly established in the Kurram Agency, a V-shaped piece of Pakistani territory that jutted into Afghanistan, about thirty-five miles southwest of Jalalabad.

The location of the weapons depot, not far from the Kurram Agency capital city Parachinar, was only a few miles away from the Afghanistan border on two sides of the V.

Obviously the ISI was using that location because of its prox-imity to mujahideen bases they were supplying across the border, which was how Sandjar had picked up the information.

According to Sandjar, the depot contained Stinger missiles as well as a whole arsenal of other weaponry, including rocket-propelled grenades and artillery shells.

This was too much of a temptation. Severinov decided to begin discussions with his 40th Army colleagues to plan an attack on the depot as soon as possible.

They would love this. The best bet was probably an aerial blitz using his favored Mi-24s, possibly with some support on the ground if needed. With any luck, he would be able to blow up half of Parachinar along with the depot.

"Worthless Pakistanis. I'm going to have you bastards," he said to himself.

* * *

Thursday, March 3, 1988
  Islamabad

It was late into the evening when TENOR finally opened the door of his apartment. Fatigue had set in after another long day of tough meetings and negotiating his way through the labyrinthine tangle of Pakistani bureaucracy—today at the Ministry of Defense.

But there remained one last task to complete before he could relax.

Like many of the informers and agents scattered across the Pakistani capital, TENOR relied on sending short encrypted messages with a burst transmitter to pass on much

of his information in between the very rare face-to-face meetings with his Russian handlers.

Many times, TENOR had wondered whether it was
worth it. He was well paid in US dollars for his main CIA job.
Did he really need to take the risks involved in supplying
information to a regime so hostile to his own?

He was the first to admit that he did it mainly because of
the money and the head rush from watching the cash pile up
in his numbered bank account in Zürich. It gave him more of
a kick than anything. He occasionally wondered why it was,
and his thoughts invariably came back to his childhood of
poverty back in Pittsburgh and the insecurities that went
with it.

Quickly he assembled his radio unit and tapped out a
message on the minuscule keyboard.

KABi FROM ISL4TENX KABi FROM ISL4TENX
SOURCES SAY CIA JOHNSON NEW MEET
WITH HASRAT PLANNED FOR JALALABADX
WILL ADVISE DATE AND ADDRESS WHEN
AVAILABLEX ENDX

Only when he had seen the red and green lights flash on
his unit, indicating a successful transmission to Severinov, did
he remove the bottle of scotch from his cupboard and pour
himself a drink.

CHAPTER NINETEEN

Thursday, March 3, 1988
Islamabad

Johnson had taken only two steps through the door of the CIA station after returning from a quiet lunch when Vic came striding up to him, waving a piece of paper.

"Our communications intercept guys have got this," Vic said.

"What?"

"It's a transcript of some encrypted burst messages about planning for an attack on the new Parrot's Beak facility near Parachinar," Vic said. Parrot's Beak was the nickname for the Kurram Agency area of Pakistan because of its geographical V shape.

"How did they get it?" Johnson asked.

"They broke the code on it last week, and they've had a feeding frenzy since. Probably won't last because the Russians will change the codes again soon."

The Agency's signals intelligence, or SIGINT, teams who

were responsible for finding new ways to intercept radio, satellite, and telephone communications had been receiving ever-increasing resources and investment in technology. They often proved their worth, as was the case now.

Vic passed the paper to Johnson, who studied it. The arms facility in the Kurram Agency had been set up as a storage and distribution base for weapons coming from the main Ojhri Camp military storage center in Rawalpindi, more than 230 miles away by road. The CIA had quietly supplied the ISI with a fleet of trucks that they used, normally during the night, to ferry weapons from Ojhri to their various satellite storage sites near the Afghanistan border for onward distribution to the mujahideen. Kurram was the newest of these sites.

"Shit," Johnson said. "That didn't take long to leak. What is it, two weeks since they set up the facility? There's a ton of Stingers and RPGs in there. Who are these messages between?"

"The intercept guys say it's between Yuri Severinov, KGB, Line PR, in Kabul, and what looks like one of his muj agents, unnamed, who must have picked it up from somewhere."

"Severinov." Johnson said. "Interesting. Haroon was talking about him a couple of days ago at our meeting. Apparently he's the guy who was responsible for the Hind raid on Hani."

Johnson read the list of messages. "So if they're aiming an assault on Parrot's Beak, it makes sense to get Javed and his guys in place with their Stingers. They can take down the Hinds from the Afghan side before they get close enough to do any damage."

"Yeah, my thoughts exactly."

"Then we can put a backup team on the Pak side as well, just in case they get past Javed," Johnson said. "But we'd better arrange to remove and disperse the weapons at the

facility too, just in case. I'm worried about Parachinar—I
don't want to see the frigging Russians destroy the city."

* * *

Wednesday, March 9, 1988
  Kurram Agency, Pakistan

Javed had not been entirely surprised to hear from Haroon
about details, derived from CIA intercepts, of a planned
Hind attack on a new ISI arms depot near Parachinar. He
was aware of the facility and had considered it a likely target
for the Russians.

He also fully agreed with Haroon's analysis: the Mi-24s
wouldn't head over the Pakistan border into the Kurram
Agency from the north—that was too obvious and too direct,
being the fastest route from Kabul. It was much more likely
they would skirt around and aim to surprise by coming from
the west.

The attack was apparently planned for three o'clock that
Wednesday. Therefore, based on map coordinates Haroon
provided, Javed, Baz, and three of his other men had spent
two days traveling to a location in the mountains just half a
mile west of the border.

Getting the location spot-on wasn't absolutely critical,
given that the Stingers had a range of perhaps five miles, but
Javed wanted to give himself the best possible chance.

They found a spot that was more than 1,500 feet above
the valley below. Height was important, because he knew the
Hinds would come in at maximum altitude to avoid any
Stingers, which were effective up to about 10,000 feet. Then
the choppers would corkscrew down rapidly, probably dropping flares, in an attempt to prevent the Stingers' infrared

tracking technology from locking onto them. By finding an elevated position from which to launch the missiles, Javed was maximizing his chances of a strike.

This time it was Baz's turn to operate the missiles. He latched Stinger tubes onto both of the gripstocks they had brought with them. Now he was ready.

Three o'clock came and went, and the only aircraft movements on either side of the border were two light planes that they saw as black specks in the distance taking off from the new military airfield at Parachinar, right across the plain that stretched out in front of them. The aircraft headed east in the direction of Islamabad.

Despite the sunshine and clear blue sky, the temperature at that altitude was hovering at around freezing. There were extensive areas of snow on the ground, which had made the climb up from the valley a tricky one. But they were used to that. Javed shivered and pulled his woolen jacket closer around him.

At just after quarter past three, Baz turned to his left. "Listen to that." As usual, Baz's acute hearing had picked up the sound first. Then he was the first to spot them too, and he pointed north.

Javed put a pair of binoculars to his eyes and focused. It was a group of three Mi-24s flying in single file at high altitude, maybe eight miles to the north of them over the 15,600-foot snow-capped peak of Mount Sikaram, heading toward the border into Pakistan.

"Baz—"

"Yes, I'm ready, don't worry. They're high, but not high enough, I don't think. And they're descending now, anyway."

"Are you sure?"

"Yes."

Baz screwed a battery coolant unit into the first Stinger, mounted it on his shoulder, and put his eye to the sight.

Then, as the choppers drew nearer, Javed eventually heard the beep as the infrared locked on.

A couple of seconds later, there was an explosion and a whoosh as the Stinger left its tube, streaking up into the azure sky. By now the choppers were more or less on the borderline.

A series of flares appeared below each of the helicopters, to the right and the left, dropping steadily, one after the other. But Javed knew that the Russian crews were a few seconds too late in pushing the flares out. By that stage, the Stinger had already locked on to the Mi-24's engine heat.

Javed watched, fascinated as always, as the missile drew a white line inexorably upward.

The lead helicopter erupted in a ball of orange with an explosive boom that echoed across the mountain range below and threw out a shower of debris that seemed to fall to earth almost in slow motion. The rear half of the aircraft, including the giant main rotor blade, had remained intact, but it flipped backward and upright, at which point the blades stopped turning and it fell, almost vertically, to the ground below.

By then, Baz already had the second Stinger on his shoulder. But just as he was raising the device to activate it against the sky, the other two choppers went into a deep, spiraling corkscrew dive, plummeting at such a rate that Javed initially thought they had also been hit.

It was a maneuver he had seen before from Mi-24 pilots coming in to land at the Jalalabad airfield in an attempt to avoid any missiles that might be aimed at them.

Baz let out a curse and tracked one of the choppers downward through his sight. Eventually, he coaxed the telltale beep out of his Stinger and fired the missile, which careered at a low, curved trajectory toward the nearer of the two remaining Mi-24s, by that stage flying well below the level at which

Javed and Baz stood, perhaps only five hundred feet above the valley floor.

Just after the missile struck the second helicopter, destroying it as well, the third bottomed out its dive extremely near to the ground. But as the pilot tried to execute a sharp turn toward the north to try to escape any more Stingers, some part of the helicopter, probably a rotor blade or the tail of the chopper—Javed wasn't sure which—touched the ground.

The chopper flipped sideways, and the rear part of the tail then hit the ground hard and broke off. The remainder of the Mi-24's fuselage spun sharply around, hit the ground again before bouncing up, and eventually came to rest near a rocky outcrop on a flat area of ground no more than a mile from where Javed was standing. Its rotors continued to turn for a minute but then gradually slowed and stopped.

Neither Javed nor Baz said anything for a few seconds. Then Baz turned, a crooked smile on his face showing multiple gaps in his teeth. "Dakh-rā Zoya!" he said. "I got all three. Allah smiled on me today!"

Javed allowed himself a grin. "Yes, he seems to smile on you every time you get that tube in your hand, Baz." He was echoing the phrase used by Baz's wife, Nazia, who tried to use humor to hide her anxiety every time her husband went out on an operation. The reference induced a loud cackle of laughter from Baz.

But Javed's mind quickly refocused on the helicopter that had crashed. He grabbed his binoculars and took a look. It seemed that most of the chopper was intact. Indeed, as he watched, the Russian crew climbed out, seemingly uninjured, and stood there for a few minutes before walking toward the mountains and the Afghan border. They were fortunate to be alive now, but they wouldn't want to be caught by Pakistani security forces or other mujahideen. If the latter got hold of them, their chances of survival were zero.

But that left the helicopter. The CIA man, Johnson, had made very clear that the Americans wanted an Mi-24 extremely badly. Badly enough to offer $50,000. This one, now inside Pakistani territory and therefore accessible, was damaged, but Javed suspected that most of the critical equipment on it was still intact. Certainly, the cockpit looked okay as far as he could see.

Javed reached inside his bag and took out a small case containing his burst radio.

CHAPTER TWENTY

Wednesday, March 9, 1988
  Islamabad

"Joe, I have some very good news," Haroon said, his voice breaking and cracking down the typically unreliable Pakistani phone line. "I have a Hind for you. Javed's men took it down near Parachinar. It has crashed, but its instruments and its weapons are all there."

Johnson, who had almost given up hope of ever obtaining either of the two big items on Langley's shopping list, had been lounging in his office chair when he picked up the receiver. But now he sat upright.

"Great," Johnson said. "Don't let any of your ISI guys near it. We'll send a transport plane up to Parachinar and take it."

"I have no doubts you will take it," Haroon said. "I am having it secured, do not worry. We will not let looters anywhere near it. But there is the small matter of getting your dollars to Javed first, in cash, and given that the Hind is on Pakistani soil, I will also need a payment. In return he will also give you the other details you were unable to discuss at Hani. He would not tell me what."

Must be the US passports, Johnson thought. *Now he's got the Hind—his big gambling chip—lined up ready to trade in.* "So he's agreed to a meeting now, suddenly?"

"Yes," Haroon said. "In Jalalabad. You can pay him for the Hind and have your discussion at the same time."

"Before, when we discussed Jalalabad, you didn't tell me how we would get there."

"I know what you're thinking," Haroon said. "But we don't need to use the Khyber. Do you know much about the Mohmand tribe?"

"A little." Johnson told Haroon he had read up on the various Pakistani and Afghan tribes as part of his intensive research before and during his posting to Islamabad. He knew the Mohmand, one of the largest, were traditionally guerrilla fighters and maverick tradesmen who liked to live by their own rules. They lived in the Federally Administered Tribal Areas of Pakistan, bordering on Afghanistan. "But how are they relevant?" he asked.

"Good, you know a bit. You'll need to learn more," Haroon said. "They're in the area thirty miles north of the Khyber, spread across both sides of the border. Some of them are smugglers. Opium, hashish, mainly. But also people. And we'll get them to smuggle you, because their area stretches right down into Goshta, just a few miles southeast of Jalalabad. They'll look after you."

"Right," Johnson said. This sounded crazy. "So you're telling me we'll go with a bunch of tribal criminals, carrying a bag of cash, and expect to get there and back safely?"

"Don't worry, Joe. It'll be fine," Haroon said.

"There'll be two of us. My colleague Vic will be coming too." He wasn't going alone, and he wouldn't give Vic a choice, although they hadn't discussed it yet.

"That's fine," Haroon said. "You'll go from the border near Sham Shah directly west to Jalalabad. It's about thirty miles from the border, and you'd have to do it by a combination of truck, mule, and maybe some of it on foot. Our Mohmand contacts use it often. We'd get a couple of them to take you. It'll be safe."

Johnson felt doubtful. "When I suggested meeting in a town or a city last time, Javed refused."

"Yes, well that was then and this is now," Haroon said. "He's changed his mind after Hani. Listen, I can see you're concerned, but you wouldn't need to go into the center of Jalalabad, which is more dangerous. There's a safe house between the airport and the river, away from security, and the guides would take you there and back out."

Haroon gave Johnson an address: Nadrees Accountants, Kumar Road. "Don't write it down, just memorize it," he said.

"How's this going to work, then?" Johnson asked.

"You dress as an Afghan, as you did for the Hani meeting, including the turban. That beard of yours works, especially when you darken your skin. I know it won't convince anyone up close, but you will be straight in and out, so it will be fine."

Johnson groaned. *It will be fine.* This operation had amateur dramatic disaster written all over it.

"When do we go?" Johnson asked.

"Friday."

The two men spent another twenty minutes discussing the fine details and the equipment required. After ending the call, Johnson walked around to Vic's office and briefed him and Neal on the latest development. To his surprise, Vic, in the same breath as moaning about the idea of Jalalabad, also volunteered to go along before Johnson could even ask him.

"I'm wondering whether we should just go without telling Watson or Jameson where we're heading," Johnson said.

"Yeah, if you want a one-way ticket straight back to Langley," Vic said. "Go right ahead." He gave Johnson a disbelieving look.

Johnson knew his friend was correct. He walked along the corridor to Watson's office on the third floor of the embassy building. Jameson was also in there, going through some papers that were spread out on Watson's desk.

After Johnson had run through the plan for Jalalabad, including the location and Vic's involvement, which Watson immediately agreed to, he sat back in his chair. "I'm just concerned about this operation leaking, like Hani," he said.

"We need to get to the bottom of what happened at Hani," Watson said. "I've asked Alec to start an inquiry into it. However, there's no need for anyone else apart from us and Vic on our side to know about Jalalabad. I'm 95 percent certain the problem is on Javed's side, as I've told you before. We can't rule out Haroon either, as his fingers seem to be in so many pies."

Johnson glanced at Jameson, who nodded in agreement. "Be extremely careful," Jameson said. "You'll get all the backup you need from us. And good luck."

* * *

Wednesday, March 9, 1988
  Kabul

Late in the evening, Severinov drained the remains of a long-cold cup of coffee and walked to his burst radio to turn it off and pack it away for the night. As he drew near, the LED on the top of the unit suddenly glowed green as it formed a connection with a transmitter elsewhere.

Severinov waited for the message to appear on the display.

KAB1 FROM ISL4TENX CONFIRMING CIA
JOHNSON MEET W/ HASRAT JALALABAD
SATURDAYX LOCATION NADREES ACCOUN-
TANTS OFFICE NEAR AIRPORTX PUT PERMA-
NENT TAIL ON HASRATX WILL ADVISE TIME
WHEN KNOWNX ENDX

So, TENOR had managed to determine a location and
date, if not a time, for the meeting between Johnson and
Javed Hasrat. That was more than useful. Severinov hadn't
even gotten around to starting his reply when, about a minute
later, the LED glowed green again as another message
arrived.

KAB1 FROM ISL4TENX HAVE SOURCED MORE
MUJ NAMES KNOWN TO HAVE SURPLUS
STINGER STOCKX 1 ROYAN SALIMOVX 2
SALAR LODIX BOTH KG PASS LOCATIONX I
ALREADY HAVE WEAPONS STOCKS
NUMBERS SUPPLIED TO BOTHX SUGGEST
IMMEDIATE ACTION AS PREVIOUSLY
DISCUSSEDX ENDX

This time, Severinov frowned. How could TENOR have
gotten hold of these mujahideen names? How did he know
they had been supplied with Stingers, and more crucially, if he
was claiming to know exact stock numbers, how did he get
hold of them? It seemed highly unlikely that the ISI would
have given them to TENOR, even if they knew, which
Severinov thought doubtful, given most ISI officers' notoriously high level of disorganization.

As he chewed over the implications, a suspicion crossed
Severinov's mind, which he then struggled to shake off. Did
the list of mujahideen coming from TENOR consist of men

to whom TENOR had sold Stingers in the first place—Stingers he now planned to sell *again* to the US under its weapons repurchasing mechanism? Maybe there was another explanation, but if true, it was an audacious scheme.

As he had previously told TENOR, he did indeed have two Spetsnaz military intelligence special forces men on his payroll, whom he could easily use for off-the-books operations such as this, providing they received an appropriate payment in return. And they were definitely not cheap.

But Severinov didn't like running operations without having a full picture in his head of what his agents and sources were doing. That was another mantra drummed into him by his father Sergo, who also had an outstanding career in the Red Army during the Second World War—the Great Patriotic War. He often told Yuri how taking care of such details had paid off while fighting against the Germans, where he was awarded the Order of the Red Banner.

Severinov mentally ran through his options. He could use the Spetsnaz operators to not only retrieve the Stingers in a series of nighttime raids but perhaps also extract information from their muj owners, before killing them, about where they had come from and who had supplied them. That might be very interesting. If they had come from TENOR originally, then Severinov might be in a position to dabble in a little blackmail sometime in the future, he mused.

Severinov checked his watch. It was almost nine o'clock. He strolled around to Rostov's office, guessing correctly that his boss, a notorious workaholic, was still in the building.

Rostov listened to Severinov's briefing carefully, then lit a cigarette and took a deep drag on it. "We can get a double win out of this. We can bring in Javed for some questioning and get out of him details of what other mujahideen have weapons in his area and where they are. That's going to buy us some massive credit with Moscow."

Severinov could almost see Rostov salivating at the thought of a promotion from his boss Anatoly Yurenko on the back of a successful operation against the muj, which would help pave the way for a trouble-free withdrawal of troops from Afghanistan in due course. He was probably even envisaging a congratulatory meeting with Gorbachev at the Kremlin.

"Then, of course," Rostov went on, tapping the end of his cigarette into his ashtray, "we need to dispose of Johnson to remove the threat of him destroying our potential side deal to sell Stingers back to the pig-brained Americans."

"Yes, Leonid," Severinov said. "It is a great opportunity." What he didn't say was that from his perspective, it might be a triple win, not just a double, if he could get Javed alone in the basement interrogation room for a few hours. He was looking forward to that most of all. It would be a chance to take revenge and at the same time to try out a few of the new toys that the KGB had installed down there.

"I don't want this to be screwed up," Rostov said. "You'll need sniper backup just in case. I'll bring the Dragunov to Jalalabad and join you."

Rostov often bragged about his expertise with his Dragunov sniper rifle and the many kills he had achieved during his army days, years earlier. Clearly he was going to try to get full credit at the Lubyanka for a successful operation by playing a hands-on part in it, Severinov mused. He was always a glory hunter, so that would be typical of him.

"Are you sure you want to get involved operationally?" Severinov asked. His boss probably hadn't fired a rifle in anger for fifteen years and couldn't possibly be as sharp as he once had been.

"Yes, of course," he said, darting one of his trademark warning glances at Severinov.

"Okay. What's your thinking on tactics?" Severinov asked.

He wasn't going to argue, but he needed to know what his boss's thoughts were, if he had any.

"This is what I've got in mind." Rostov began to run through the outline of his plan.

* * *

Thursday, March 10, 1988
  Islamabad

"I need a backup plan, Jayne," Johnson said as he took another sip from his third glass of scotch, each of them large doubles. "Those guys are like men made of smoke. You can't pin them down."

He had spent the previous hour with Jayne running through his plan for the Jalalabad trip and the indefinable concern he had that when the chips were down, he couldn't rely on Watson and Jameson to act swiftly and decisively if needed. Would he still be here to tell the tale if they had been left to coordinate the helicopter rescue at Hani instead of her? He was certain the answer was no.

Jayne walked over to the table in Johnson's apartment and poured herself another vodka, also a large double, which was her fourth.

Having had the apartment swept for bugs yet again the previous day, Johnson now felt more at ease about having her around for the evening. He knew she had taken every precaution to avoid surveillance by the ISI or anyone else on the way there.

Moreover, if he was going to put himself on the firing line over the next few days, then he was damn well going to enjoy himself for a couple of hours beforehand.

"I'll do what I can, Joe," Jayne said. "We've got two assets in Jalalabad now on the mujahideen side. If needed, I can mobilize them. Two of them are Massoud's guys." She smiled. Johnson knew there was a lot of undercover maneuverings going on between MI6 and Ahmad Shah Massoud, the Tajik mujahideen who had been leading the fight against the Russians. Massoud had been dubbed the Lion of Panjshir after his heroics in his home region of the Panjshir Valley.

"But we're not going to be able to get a chopper into Jalalabad," she added.

"I know that, obviously," Johnson said. He removed from his belt the Beretta M9 that he had taken from the weapons locker at the CIA station and placed it on the arm of the sofa next to him.

Jayne came back to the sofa and sat next to Johnson, then crossed her legs and turned sideways to face him directly, her right arm resting on the back of the sofa, holding her glass.

"What got you into this job?" she asked. "Your motivation, your drive—where did it come from?"

"I thought it would be an opportunity to work against some of the darker forces that exist on the planet," Johnson said. "Never going to win the battle, but someone's got to try." He went on to detail the ordeal his mother had gone through at the hands of the Nazis in Gross-Rosen as something that had always inspired him.

"But we—you, me, all of us—don't exactly always operate in the light ourselves, do we?" Jayne asked.

"Usually somewhere in the gray," Johnson said. "And there's a lot of gray areas in our job. Fighting black with white is a nonstarter."

Jayne laughed. "You're right there."

From what Johnson had observed of Jayne in the brief time they had been together, he definitely liked her down-to-earth sense of humor and her grasp of reality.

She bent down, put her glass on the floor, and smiled at him.

Nodding toward the Beretta, she said, "Glad to see you're taking precautions, Joe."

She let her hand slip forward from the back of the sofa until it was touching his shoulder and let it rest there for a few minutes while they continued talking.

Then when the conversation lulled, she leaned toward him and kissed him, full and gently, on the lips. After a couple of seconds, she moved her head back a little and looked him in the eyes.

"Common sense tells me not to do that, but I've wanted to for a while," Jayne said. "Ever since that evening at Dennis's."

Johnson tried not to show his slight feeling of surprise. He nodded and put his hand on her shoulder. "Yes, common sense, the CIA part of my brain, tells me the same—but screw that, I've also wanted to." He leaned toward her and kissed her again. This time her lips parted, and he nibbled first at her bottom lip, then her top one before she responded by slowly slipping her tongue inside his mouth.

Jayne slid sideways and moved her left leg so it was resting on top of his thigh, then drew a line at a tantalizingly slow speed with her forefinger up the inside of his thigh as she kissed him.

Johnson put his right hand at the back of her neck and pulled her closer, suddenly feeling intoxicated. It had been almost a year since he had last kissed a woman like this and made love, when he was at home on vacation.

"Do you want to stay here tonight?" Johnson whispered in her ear after twenty minutes of almost uninterrupted kissing.

"Not tonight," Jayne said. "You need to get up at five o'clock, don't you? But let's see how things go when you're back from Jalalabad." She paused and stroked his cheek. "That's me being far too sensible again, isn't it?"

"Yup," Johnson said.

"You need some sleep before this operation, not me keeping you up all night, so to speak," Jayne giggled. "Am I right or wrong?"

Johnson groaned. "You're probably right. I guess you've just given me an incentive to come back."

PART FOUR

CHAPTER TWENTY-ONE

Friday, March 11, 1988
Pakistan-Afghanistan border, Mohmand Agency

The 165-mile route from Islamabad to the tiny village of Sham Shah near the Afghanistan border took more than seven hours, much of it along gray, dusty, potholed roads crammed with overloaded trucks, carts pulled by mules, rusty bicycles, and battered cars.

Johnson and Vic, sitting in the rear seats of a dented and heavily scratched double-cab Toyota pickup truck, spoke little as the driver, a Pashtun employed by the CIA, piloted them northeast. They skirted Peshawar to the north and then headed over the mountains to Ghalanai, the main town of the Mohmand Agency, which nestled in a natural bowl surrounded by towering peaks on all sides.

Outside the agency hospital in Ghalanai, a low-slung single-story cream and terra-cotta building, they picked up their guide, Elam Durrani, a straight-backed Pashtun with high cheekbones and a gray-flecked beard, who spoke good English.

Johnson, who was wearing a white turban with a gray *shalwar kameez* and jacket, learned from Elam that most of the journey from the border to Jalalabad would be by pickup truck. However, there was a stretch of ten miles through a mountain gorge where they would need to travel by mule. They set off again, heading past men running rickety wooden stalls selling everything from car tires to walnuts to vegetables and cooking oil. Women wearing burkas fussed over groups of children.

The battered CIA pickup blended seamlessly with the other vehicles on the road, although Johnson reflected that its highly tuned engine was undoubtedly in a somewhat better condition and its new tires contrasted with the threadbare versions generally in use.

As they drove, the backdrop of the Hindu Kush mountains rose—dark, moody, and threatening—ahead of them.

Johnson was tempted to smile when he saw the Pakistan border post, which was just a small concrete hut in the middle of nowhere, flying the national flag next to a rough track that led from the Mohmand Agency into the neighboring Afghanistan district of Goshta. There was nothing to stop locals from freely moving from one side to the other. According to Elam, they were virtually all from the Mohmand tribe, anyway.

"This is a smuggler's paradise," Elam said. "Anything you want—opium, hashish, guns—these guys can get it," he said, indicating toward a line of six small trucks waiting at the side of the road, all laden with plain wooden boxes full of unknown contraband.

Johnson, who had $25,000 in used US bills hidden in the false bottom of his backpack, said nothing. The other $25,000 was in Vic's pack.

Behind the final truck, a man was taking Kalashnikovs from a wooden box and laying them out on the ground. A line of men stood and watched, their eyes shifting between the man with the guns and the border post.

Johnson, who had been holding the Beretta tucked inside the folds of his *shalwar kameez*, almost reflexively removed the magazine and checked it was full, even though he knew it was. He then racked the slide unobtrusively and flipped the safety off, then back on again. The simple process somehow made him feel more secure.

Vic, who also carried an M9, watched Johnson with some mild amusement. "Do you want a smoke? Then you might stop fiddling with your hands," he said.

Elam counted out a sheaf of banknotes, stuffed them in his pocket, and jumped out of the Toyota at the border post. He disappeared into the hut and emerged again two minutes later with a grin on his face. "Okay, we can go," he said. Johnson didn't ask how much the bribe had cost. None of them were asked to show their passports.

"We will need to keep watch for any Afghan army patrols or helicopters, which obviously the Russians are controlling," Elam said. "But the guy in there said there are none around at the moment."

After traveling a few miles into Afghanistan along a flat plain flanked on either side by mountains, they came to a few small settlements, most of which seemed deserted. Fields that had clearly been cultivated at one point were now over-grown with two-meter-high grasses and bushes. Irrigation canals were blocked with silt, and many of their containing walls were broken.

"Where are all the villagers?" Vic asked Elam.

"All fled because of the hostile environment the Russians have created around here," Elam said. "Most of them have become refugees and gone over the border to Pakistan, living in the Mohmand Agency. They're mainly Mohmand people, anyway. The only business here at the moment is smuggling drugs and weapons. I know of some people who have gone much farther—overseas if they can. The US, the UK—they try to get refugee status there."

About ten miles into Afghanistan, Elam brought the pickup to a halt next to a shack with mud walls and a distinctive bridge over a broad stream. Johnson gazed at the bridge, which had two wooden carvings of eagles at each end.

"That bridge seems out of place," Johnson said to Vic.

"What do you mean?" Vic asked.

"It looks completely over-ornate in such a deserted rural location," Johnson said. Next to the bridge about ten mules were grazing in a paddock.

His attention was distracted by Elam, who pointed to a rickety wooden shed. "The pickup goes in there, and this is where we switch to mules," he said. "The track beyond here is either tractor or mule transport. And nobody's got a tractor anymore because the Russians have taken them all. We sleep here tonight, then on to Jalalabad tomorrow morning."

Johnson and Vic looked at each other.

"Have you ridden a mule before?" Elam asked.

"Yes," Johnson said. "I rode one a couple of weeks ago—very briefly and very badly. Apart from that, only as a kid."

* * *

Saturday, March 12, 1988
  Jalalabad

The three-hour mule trek through the mountain gorge northward through the Goshta District toward Jalalabad had taken its toll on Johnson, whose backside had been rubbed raw in places by the rigid leather saddle. To compound the discomfort, his back was also stiff from a night spent sleeping on a rubber mat on a dirt floor.

As they climbed into another aged pickup truck that Elam had retrieved from a shed, Johnson reflected bitterly to Vic that none of this had featured in the CIA's training at "the Farm." He was referring to Camp Peary, the Agency's covert training facility near Williamsburg, Virginia, where he and Vic had learned tradecraft as new agents.

Three times during the mule trek a pair of military helicopters had flown overhead, patrolling the mountain pass. Upon hearing them approaching, Elam on each occasion had made Johnson and Vic dismount from the mules and cover themselves in gray blankets up against nearby rocks.

The woolen cloth was virtually the same color as the surrounding stony gray ground and, Elam said, made a person almost impossible to spot from the air.

Second, the blankets acted as thermal insulation, making it harder for infrared equipment to pick up their image. That would work only for a short period, but it was generally long enough to remain undetected while a chopper flew past.

"It works. It is a mujahideen tactic," Elam said.

He was proved correct. At no point did the choppers come for a closer look and instead clattered onward at speed toward the Pakistan border.

"What about the mules?" Johnson asked.

"Don't worry. They just assume they're out grazing," Elam said. Johnson wasn't reassured. He hadn't seen many others wandering loose.

Johnson was surprised not to have seen more of a military presence on the ground. He had been expecting to have to skirt around Russian checkpoints, but hadn't seen any. Perhaps this was an early indicator that the Soviets really were preparing for a withdrawal from Afghanistan, he wondered.

A shriveled man with a curved spine emerged from behind the shed that had housed the pickup and took their mules. Elam explained that he would look after the animals until they returned for the journey back into Pakistan.

As they drew nearer to the village of Goshta, the dirt road became busier with the occasional tractor, truck, and pickup alongside the mule carts and villagers carrying bundles of firewood and vegetables.

Then suddenly, in front of them, was the vast expanse of the Kabul River, flowing eastward in the direction of Pakistan, where it eventually became part of the Indus.

Because there was no bridge crossing from Goshta to Jalalabad or the airport, which lay only fourteen miles upstream to the west, the only option by road to their destination was a tortuous route of more than thirty miles that would take almost two hours. That meant using bridges farther upstream and then driving down through the center of Jalalabad to the airport on the south side.

After a detailed debate, Johnson and Vic agreed with Elam that they should instead park the pickup on the Goshta side of the river and use a boat owned by one of Elam's trusted contacts to cross. That would be far quicker, as the boat could get them very close to the safe house meeting place, which lay on a patch of land just a mile wide between the airport and the river. It would also avoid several military checkpoints close to Jalalabad and facilitate a more rapid and less predictable escape route back toward the Pakistan border if required.

Therefore, after driving fifteen miles toward Jalalabad, Elam cut left down a steep track toward the river, where he parked next to a wooden boathouse.

"My friend here is going to take us," Elam said. "I won't

give you his name—he is already under surveillance by the KHAD."

Fifteen minutes later, they were heading diagonally eastward across the river in an old inflatable motorboat with an engine that spluttered occasionally.

"It sounds like a goddamn chain-smoker with asthma," Vic whispered to Johnson. "It's not going to get us out of trouble in a hurry."

The boat owner had handed each of them fishing rods, and to the casual observer they appeared to be a group of friends out to catch their dinner.

"We will sit on a jetty where people sometimes fish and try to catch something until it is time for the meeting," Elam said. "It builds a cover story and is a tactic we have used before. Then we can walk to the safe house."

Sure enough, after tying up the boat at a jetty, they found a handful of other men using it as a fishing spot from where they could cast into a stretch of the Kabul River that was deep but slow moving. Elam chose a spot well away from the other men, most of whom wore ancient *shalwar kameezes* and looked cripplingly poor. The river water, consisting of melted snow that had drained straight off the Hindu Kush, was hand-numbingly cold.

Twice Johnson noticed Afghan police cars that drove behind them past the jetty, the officer in the passenger seat staring at the fishermen from his open window. But neither car stopped.

Haroon had set the meeting time for eighteen minutes past two in the afternoon, when he figured the security forces around Jalalabad were likely to be either eating lunch or dozing off. Johnson approved of the timing. Using a time either on the hour or half hour was too obvious and formal.

At three minutes past two, Johnson glanced at Elam. "Time to move," he said.

Elam nodded and jerked his thumb toward the boat owner. "He will wait here with the boat and the fishing rods. I will take you to the safe house and wait nearby for you to finish."

Johnson's surveillance antennae had been on an adrenaline-fueled high since their arrival at the jetty. He had carried out a thorough visual check on all the other fishermen as well as a few apparently casual locals hanging around slightly farther up the street that led past fields and buildings toward the airport.

The street was lined on one side by a concrete drainage ditch that ran into the river. Every so often there were small bridges across the ditch to allow vehicles to pass to another road that ran parallel to it.

Nothing he could see gave cause for special concern. There were no cars or trucks loitering with people waiting inside. Nobody who didn't seem part of a legitimate group or without a purpose. Yet some primeval sixth sense kept nagging away at the back of his mind.

"What feeling are you getting here, Vic?" he asked.

Vic looked at him sharply. "Looks okay to me. I've checked everyone."

"Yes, I know it looks okay. But it's how it feels that isn't quite right."

Vic shrugged. "We don't have an option now."

CHAPTER TWENTY-TWO

Saturday, March 12, 1988
  Jalalabad

The safe house was a small gray office building on the southern side of the street, with a sign outside that said Nadrees Accountants. Johnson and Vic carried out one final check for surveillance, using the ritual of lighting and smoking a cigarette as cover.

Satisfied that all was clear, Johnson told Elam to remain outside the Nadrees building to keep a watch while he and Vic went down an alleyway to the rear. Following Haroon's instructions, they entered through a green wooden door that had been left ajar.

They found themselves in a basic kitchen, with a square table and chairs in the center, a stainless steel sink, a counter made of plywood, a rusting electric stove with a black kettle on it, and an ancient fridge that was making a faint hissing noise. The concrete floor was heavily stained in places with brown and red blotches, and a single bare light bulb hung from a hook in the center of the ceiling. The windows were barred with several vertical lengths of steel.

Johnson, with one hand on the Beretta concealed in his belt beneath his *shalwar kameez*, knocked on the table three times as arranged and waited.

Almost immediately, they heard faint footsteps from behind the half-open door that led from the kitchen, and to Johnson's relief, the figure of Javed appeared. Behind him, two other men followed, one of whom disappeared again almost immediately.

Javed gave a grin of recognition and strode to Johnson, hand outstretched. "So, you are also still alive. Let's hope we have more success this time than we had in Hani."

"Yes, indeed," Johnson said. He introduced Vic, and Javed did likewise with his remaining colleague, Baz.

Javed walked to the exterior door through which Johnson and Vic had entered and locked it with two steel bolts. Then he led the way to another room, laid out with four sofas around a low, square wooden table, where he poured chai for all of them.

"Let's do the main business first," Johnson said. "The helicopter and the money."

Noting that Javed had a burst radio on a table in the corner of the room, he removed his own from his backpack and quickly assembled it. During a discussion over the first cup of chai, which Baz poured into small glasses and offered with a rough lump of sugar, they agreed that Javed would send a message to Haroon to confirm payment. Haroon would then instruct his ISI colleagues to release the crippled Mi-24 in Kurram Agency to the CIA team that was retrieving it.

At the same time, Johnson would confirm via a burst transmission to Jameson that the transaction was complete and that the team dispatched to Kurram was clear to remove the Hind.

Ten minutes later, the deal was done, Haroon confirmed the handover was authorized, and Johnson handed over the money, which Javed carefully counted. "Good," Javed said, with barely concealed satisfaction. "You have your chopper and I have my money. What about my passport and visas?"

"Yes," Johnson said. "But first, let's make some progress on the Stinger distribution issue. You told me you have only a few left?"

"Yes, we had five, but now there's just three after Baz shot down the Mi-24s in Kurram," Javed said, inclining his head toward Baz.

"What about other muj commanders?"

"In my region some of the mujahideen have stocks, and they have fairly recently acquired more."

"I need names," Johnson said impatiently. "And locations."

Javed hesitated. "This information is not being supplied by me," he said, studying Johnson carefully.

"Of course, agreed. Go on."

"In the K-G Pass area, Royan Salimov, a Tajik, has a large number, I am told," Javed said, with a glance at Baz. "Salar Lodi, a Pashtun, also has many." He leaned back in his chair.

"So have these come from the ISI?" Johnson asked. "Our mutual friend told me that there have been other sources too."

"Yes, I know that a proportion of those Stingers came from an American supplier."

Now Johnson felt he was getting somewhere. And Javed was prepared to talk too.

"So who is this American?" Johnson asked. "A business-man? An arms dealer? Who?"

Javed scratched at his thick beard and twirled his fore-finger around in a circle in the same gesture that Johnson remembered him making at their previous meeting. Javed shook his head slowly. "I gave my word to the person who gave me the information that I would not disclose that. It will put him in a great deal of difficulty if I do that, in fact in some danger, I am guessing."

Johnson sighed inwardly. Was Javed just playing games? Haroon had warned him that this might happen. He decided to start with the moral argument.

"The thing is," Johnson said, "we are all in a war here, and I see a lot of people suffering, mainly poor Afghans who get caught up innocently in all the shit that's going on. Russians are bombing these people out of their homes. But I also see a small minority of people making money out of this suffering, and that's acceptable and unavoidable sometimes. Like you— you've just made a fortune from us, but that's fair enough given the risks you took. But if a presumably rich arms-dealing American is working ad hoc supplying antiaircraft missiles to mujahideen in some kind of freelance, uncon-trolled operation, it's damned dangerous. If the Russians find out, we're all going to be history, you realize that? If the Kremlin gets hard proof of what's going on, the whole Afghan program will be scrapped prematurely, and the United States will look like a joke. Your flow of money will be dead, and I'll be out of a job, probably, along with all my colleagues. It'll be carnage."

Javed wrinkled his eyes, appearing to wrestle with the argument. "I can't," he said eventually.

Johnson decided to push the only remaining button he had left. "If you want the US passports and visas, you'll need to tell me who the American is who supplied the weapons."

Javed looked up at Baz, who was standing near the door, and raised an eyebrow. Baz inclined his head toward the door, indicating to Javed to come with him. The muj leader got to his feet. "Excuse me, I will be back in a minute," he said. He followed Baz out the door.

Johnson glanced at Vic. "What do you think? Any chance?" he asked.

"They're at least discussing it."

Johnson leaned back in his chair and briefly looked at the ceiling, which was covered with cobwebs, a few water stains, and several dark patches.

Then the door handle rattled and back came Javed and Baz, the former carrying a small rectangular piece of paper. He walked to the table and put it down in front of Johnson, who bent forward to look at it.

It was a grainy black-and-white photograph of a man in front of a mule cart. The picture seemed to have been snapped without the subject's knowledge, as there were other men in the way. The man next to the cart was carrying a Stinger missile tube, which he appeared to be handing over to an Afghan in a turban. There were more Stingers visible on the back of the cart, and in the background, behind the man with the Stinger, was another Westerner, a taller, thicker-set bearded man also holding a Stinger.

The men were standing next to a bridge, which also caught Johnson's eye.

He felt his bowel turn over as he scrutinized the picture.

"Let's have a look," Vic said. He took the photograph from Johnson. "Well, fuck me," he said.

He turned it over. On the back was written one word in capital letters. TENOR. "What the hell is this?"

The man with the Stinger was Robert Watson. And the taller figure behind him Johnson recognized as the man from Kay Associates whom he had seen visiting Watson at the CIA station a few weeks earlier.

The bridge next to which the men were standing had two ornate carved wooden eagles at either end. It was the same one Johnson and Vic had noticed on their way into

Afghanistan after they had crossed the border from the Mohmand Agency.

"Who's the tall man standing at the back?" Johnson asked, his voice rising sharply.

Javed shrugged. "I don't know."

Johnson pressed his lips together. This was dynamite. "Where did you get this photo?"

"It belongs to a friend. Another mujahideen," Javed said. "It's a copy—Baz and I are keeping it safe for him."

"Why does he have it?"

"It's a precaution. It's proof—in case the Americans delivering the Stingers turn nasty."

Johnson and Vic looked up from the photograph as the man who they had seen briefly upon their arrival earlier came into the room. He approached Javed and whispered something.

"Excuse me, I need to go and discuss an issue," Javed said, gesturing toward his colleague. They left the room, leaving the door open.

Johnson could hear them muttering in the hallway outside. Now all his instincts were flashing red alert again. "There's something wrong here," he said to Vic, who grimaced.

Soon afterward, Javed returned, walking briskly. "My surveillance team has been told by a source that the KGB may know about this meeting. You should leave now, just in case that is true."

Johnson stood. "Son of a bitch. Unbelievable," he said, glancing at Vic.

"Yes, it is unbelievable," Javed said. "Only Baz and I knew about this meeting on our side. I have kept it utterly quiet and confidential because of the risks." He stared at Johnson. "I hope you took similar precautions. But we haven't got time to discuss that now."

"No, we haven't," Johnson said. "Let's get the hell out of here, then." He nodded at Javed. "We'll be in contact and we'll sort out the passports and visas. Thanks. Can I take this photo?" He pointed to the picture of Watson.

Javed shook his head, picked up the photo, and pocketed it.

CHAPTER TWENTY-THREE

Saturday, March 12, 1988
Jalalabad

Javed pushed Johnson toward the door. "You must go," he said, his eyes flashing black.

"Can't I just take the photo?" Johnson said. "I need—"

"I said no," Javed said, his tone now abrasive and loud. "That's final. My colleague needs it, for the reason I explained. But I will get a copy sent to you through Haroon. I promise I'll send it, and I thank you in advance for the passports and visas—I trust you will keep your word on that. Go with Baz here; he will take you out."

He pushed Johnson again.

Johnson grimaced and began to reach into his bag for his camera. "But it's important. Can I instead take a photograph of it? I think it's quite—"

"No, just go!" Javed snapped. "You're wasting time."

Baz beckoned them, and they ran out through the kitchen, where Baz unbolted the rear door and, after checking the yard, led the way back into the alley at the side of the property. The dust-blown street was quiet, and Elam was sitting a few yards away on a concrete post.

"Is everything okay?" Elam asked, jumping to his feet.

"No, it's not," Johnson said, signaling with his hand toward the river. "We need to move fast. The Russians found out about the meeting." He turned and shook Baz's hand. "Good luck, and remember to tell Javed to send a copy of that photo," he said.

Moving at a fast walk, Johnson led the way back down the street toward the jetty, which he estimated was about two-thirds of a mile away. After several minutes, they had covered half of that when they came to another of the small road bridges that crossed the drainage ditch.

As Johnson had done previously, he carefully checked the junction on the other side of the bridge, where there was a row of gray cement office buildings with narrow alleyways between them.

Then, hearing a distant squeal of brakes, he glanced back up the street behind them. Two black cars had pulled to a halt just outside the building they had exited. Four men dressed in black piled out of the car and ran into the building. This didn't look good. Another car barreled down the road behind them and also screeched to a stop.

"Shit. Hope Javed got out of there," Johnson said.

Vic, who had also turned in time to see the drama unfold, cursed. "KGB, has to be. Bastards. We'd better get going, else they'll be down here for us."

Johnson, adrenaline now pumping, turned and looked around the street. That was when he saw the man, dressed in black and wearing a black *chitrali* cap, and standing perhaps eighty yards away. On his shoulder he had a rifle that was pointed in their direction.

Instinct took over. Johnson shouted, "Move!" and shoved

Vic and Elam into the recessed doorway of the industrial building outside which they were standing.

He followed them a split second later, hearing a loud whine and feeling a sharp sting on the top of his right ear as he did so. A spray of cement exploded from the wall next to him, and then came a crash as a chunk of masonry fell to the ground.

"Shit," Johnson muttered. He put his hand to his ear and pushed the other men farther into the recess as he tried to give himself more cover. As he did so, another bullet smashed into the cement wall next to him. A third followed, cannoning with a deafening clang into the large steel shutter covering a vehicle entrance to the building, next to the doorway where they were sheltering.

Johnson looked at his right hand; it was covered in blood. "They've frigging hit me," he said. "Is that door unlocked?"

Vic pulled down on the handle of the wooden door behind him, and it creaked open.

"Go through, quick," Johnson said. "Maybe we can get out the back." He pulled his Beretta from under his *shalwar kameez* and clicked off the safety, now feeling the warm trickle of blood down the side of his face. Vic also took out his handgun.

Closing and locking the door to the street behind them, the three men looked around. They were in a warehouse building that appeared abandoned. There were several steel tables standing on the concrete floor, all covered in dust, with bundles of brown paper next to them, and a few high metal shelving units lined the walls, but that was about it. Maybe this had once been some kind of packing operation, Johnson thought.

The building, about forty yards long, was built in an L shape, with part of the far end of the warehouse out of sight around a corner to the right.

"Let's get down the other end," Johnson said. "Maybe there's a rear door out of here."

The three men dodged around the tables and ran to the far end of the building and round to the right. As they did so, two bullets smashed in quick succession through the wooden front door through which they had just entered.

There was a rear door to the property positioned around the corner, out of sight of the front door, but it was locked. Johnson gave it a sharp kick with the bottom of his shoe. It shuddered but didn't give in. Now the blood coming from his ear was dripping steadily off his chin and onto the floor.

"All of you, kick together. One, two, three . . . " The three men simultaneously planted the flats of their feet hard against the door, but it didn't move.

From the front of the property, another series of gunshots hammered into the door.

Johnson looked around. There were two windows on either side of the door, but both had four thick steel bars screwed firmly into the window ledge. They were obviously designed to prevent intruders from getting in, but they also now prevented Johnson, Vic, and Elam from getting out.

"Shit," Johnson said. From the front of the property came a loud protracted creak as the front door opened slowly. "He's coming in."

CHAPTER TWENTY-FOUR

Saturday, March 12, 1988
  Jalalabad

"You keep trying the door," Johnson said to Vic and Elam. "See if you can find something to smash it open. I'll give you some cover."

There came the brief sound of footsteps echoing from the far end of the warehouse; then they stopped.

"Just kill him," Elam whispered.

Johnson hesitated. "You just keep trying that door." He sprinted to the corner of the L shape and scrambled behind one of the metal tables, all of which had shelving underneath made from solid steel sheets, giving him some protection.

He wriggled to the corner of the table and peered around, his Beretta at the ready. Blood from his injured ear was continuing to drip down his face, drenching the top half of his *shalwar kameez*.

The building was suddenly silent, but Johnson's mind was racing. If this was KGB, then surely they would have backup outside somewhere. Unless, of course, it was a lone operator detailed to carry out a fingerprint-free killing of US diplomatic staff on Afghan soil with no witnesses, which might give the KGB more deniability than if several officers were involved.

Or was it not KGB but some kind of kidnap attempt?

What is this guy going to do?

Johnson gradually raised himself up until he could see more of the warehouse. From behind him came a loud bang, followed by another. He turned his head briefly to look. Vic had a crowbar in his hand, and Elam a length of what looked like metal scaffolding, which he was using to batter the wooden rear door.

Johnson refocused on trying to spot the gunman. Unless they could get the door open immediately, his plan A, to escape without shooting the guy, would have to be rapidly revised.

At one side of a table near to the front door, Johnson caught a glimpse of black clothing, which then immediately disappeared. A few seconds later there came two successive gunshots and deafening clangs as bullets smashed into the steel table in front of Johnson.

Johnson flinched in surprise, distracting him from his focus on the table behind which the gunman was hiding. As a result, when the man then moved from behind that table to another one a few yards farther to the right along the warehouse floor, Johnson missed his chance to get a shot in.

"Shit," Johnson muttered. He could tell from their sound that the rounds were from a pistol, not the rifle that the man had been using outside. *He must have two guns.*

The gunman now had a better angle to potentially fire at Vic and Elam, who were still bashing away at the door behind him. Now Johnson definitely had no choice but to go on the offensive.

He forced himself to ignore his bleeding ear and the banging from behind and to concentrate. He risked a quick look and noticed the very top of the man's *chitrali* cap protruding above the table behind which he was hiding.

The cap was scarcely visible—there was probably no more than half an inch showing. Johnson aimed his Beretta at it carefully. He consciously slowed his breathing and then gently squeezed the trigger.

The round, the first that Johnson had fired, whined over the tabletop and clipped the cap. It must have surprised the gunman, who moved just enough to inadvertently show part of his left shoulder at the side of the table, but before Johnson could get a shot off, he moved again, and the shoulder was no longer visible.

Simultaneously, Johnson sprinted at a crouch to another table a few yards to his right. As he ducked down, there came two shots from the gunman. One of the rounds clanged into the table where Johnson had previously been hiding; the other hit the wall.

After a few seconds, Johnson peered around the side of the table. As he had hoped, the new wider angle enabled him to see a little of the man's body; three or four inches of his left shoulder were exposed.

Johnson raised his Beretta and carefully fired a round. The man recoiled and grunted and rolled reflexively to his left, revealing his head, and Johnson immediately took aim and pulled the trigger once more.

The man's head jerked back. He rolled over and lay still, facedown.

Johnson ran to the man, covering him with his Beretta the whole way. When he was convinced the man was not going to move, he quickly approached and turned him over. The round had clipped him on the front right side of his temple, removing a chunk of flesh and leaving a glimpse of white bone beneath. The wound was bleeding heavily, and he was unconscious.

That was when Johnson started back in surprise. He knew the face. It was the same man whose photo Alec Jameson had shown him back in the CIA station in Islamabad: Leonid Rostov, head of the KGB's Line PR military intelligence operation in Afghanistan.

What the hell is an intelligence chief doing out on the street getting into gun battles?

Johnson grabbed the pistol from Rostov's right hand, a Makarov, and felt his pulse, which was weak but still there. There was no sign of a rifle. Briefly, Johnson considered putting a bullet through Rostov's head to finish him off but decided against it.

He turned just in time to see Vic use the scaffolding tube to hammer the end of the crowbar, which Elam had rammed into the crack between the door frame and the door.

With a screech of steel and splintering wood, the rear door of the warehouse finally burst open.

Johnson ran over to Vic. "I hit the bastard in the head. It's Rostov—the KGB boss."

"*Rostov?* You sure? Is he dead?" Vic asked.

"Definitely him. Not dead but will be. Head wound and unconscious," Johnson said. "Come on. Let's get the hell out of here."

CHAPTER TWENTY-FIVE

Saturday, March 12, 1988
Jalalabad

A white light flashed across Javed's vision as the fist crashed into his temple, sending his head jerking back. Another blow struck him on the left side of the head. Then someone shoved him hard in the back and he went sprawling onto the damp floor of the dark, stinking cell.

Behind him, the metal door of the cell clanged shut. Javed turned over and sat on the floor, looking up through the gloom at the two Russians who stood on either side of the cell door.

After ambushing him as he tried to escape from the rear of the safe house—one group coming in through the front, another waiting on some rough ground behind the property —the KGB infidels had taken him in a van to the KHAD offices near the Jalalabad airport. There had been no sight of Baz there. Hopefully he had somehow escaped as the Soviets had arrived.

"You mujahideen piece of shit," said the taller of the two men, standing on the right. "You need to start talking, now." The man squatted on his haunches, running a hand through dark, wiry hair. "You don't know who I am, do you?"

"No," Javed said.

"Good. All you need to know is that I'm KGB. We know your record, your murderous activities against our troops and helicopters in this country. And now we know you've been meeting with American spies. What I want to know is, where did they go?"

Javed stared at the man and said nothing. He had no intention of saying anything, although he knew that the consequences of doing so would be hard to bear.

The meeting with Johnson had been kept absolutely watertight on his side. So how the hell the KGB had found out about his meeting with Johnson and his colleague, Javed had no idea, although in truth, he wasn't entirely surprised. The country and neighboring Pakistan, were so stuffed full with agents, double agents, and probably triple agents, it was dangerous to talk to anyone about anything.

Javed felt he had done his best to give Johnson, Vic, and Elam the best possible chance of escaping by keeping his mouth shut, both at the safe house when the KGB had burst in and again now.

"I said, we know you've been meeting with American spies here," the Russian said, his voice rising. "Admit it. Confess. Where did they go, and when did they go?"

Again, Javed said nothing.

The Russian took a step toward him and let fly with a kick that smashed into Javed's ribs, despite his attempt to deflect it by raising his forearm. The blow knocked him sideways to the floor. Then came another kick straight into the kidneys that left Javed dizzy with pain.

He groaned, and the KGB man stamped on his

outstretched right hand, crushing his fingers against the hard floor.

"I know what you did in January in the Khost-Gardez Pass," he said. "The Stinger attack on our helicopters—and then what you did afterward to the crew." His voice was cold and hard. "Tell me about it. Admit it."

Javed shook his head, his mind racing. How did this Russian know of his involvement in the K-G Pass attack?

"Don't worry," the Russian said, taking a step backward. "If you're not going to speak, you won't be here long. You'll be going to a much nicer place."

Now what was he talking about? Javed lifted his head off the floor and tried to sit up again, glancing at the man.

"You'll be going to Pul-e-Charkhi later," the Russian said. "I'll look forward to carrying on our conversation there, where I have more toys at my disposal that might encourage you to loosen your tongue. And don't worry—you will talk. I'll make sure of that."

Javed grimaced. Pul-e-Charkhi was the Soviet-controlled prison in Kabul, notorious for the savage tortures carried out by KHAD intelligence officers under the direction of the KGB. He had heard sickening stories about some of the techniques employed. Death rates at the prison were sky high and disease and malnutrition rife, partly due to the overcrowding.

There was a knock at the door of the cell. A man put his head around the door and spoke to the KGB officer in rapid Russian. Javed picked up enough of the conversation to gather that someone called Rostov had been shot while pursuing the Americans.

The KGB man cursed violently, then spat on the floor. "I warned him not to do that. The idiot," he muttered to the man.

If he hadn't been in so much pain, Javed would have smiled. He didn't know exactly who Rostov was, and he wasn't going to ask for clarification, although he recalled Haroon mentioning the name when they were discussing KGB officers who had been coordinating attacks on Afghan villages. But it clearly mattered to this Russian. And the CIA agents appeared to have gotten away. That was the only bit of good news coming out of the afternoon's debacle.

CHAPTER TWENTY-SIX

Sunday, March 13, 1988
Islamabad

For the fifth time, the sound of fast-approaching helicopters echoed across the mountain gorge, and for the fifth time, Johnson scrambled off his mule and took a gray Afghan blanket from his backpack. He dived as close as he could to the nearest large rock and used the blanket to cover himself as best he could.

Vic and Elam were doing likewise a few yards away.

The rapid rhythmic thundering of the chopper engines grew louder and nearer, until Johnson could tell they were directly overhead. There were at least two, maybe three of them again, as on the previous patrol. This time he hadn't stopped to look and count.

It seemed inevitable that one of the Russian military patrols would spot them, surely. They had been running up and down the mountain gorge at intervals for the past hour or so, flying as low as the terrain would allow. It seemed certain to Johnson that these patrols had been specifically detailed to track down him and Vic.

As with the inward journey, Elam instructed Johnson and Vic to use the blankets as a simple cover whenever the helicopters approached. Again this tactic seemed to work. Maybe, Johnson thought, that was partly because the temperature had dropped several degrees since their infiltration into Afghanistan and he was now so damn freezing that the likelihood of showing up on an infrared detector was minimal. At least that was how he felt.

The first helicopter patrol seemed to Johnson to hover above them for an age. But eventually they buzzed off into the distance, the racket from their engines gradually fading. After they had gone, Johnson, as he had done previously, folded the blanket and replaced it in his small backpack.

The top of his right earlobe continued to throb from the bullet wound. It had taken more than an hour of continuous firm pressure, using a strip ripped from the bottom of his *shalwar kameez* as a makeshift bandage, before the bleeding had stopped. Johnson could feel that the round had removed a piece of flesh as it had whined past. But as Vic kept reminding him, another inch and he would have been dead. It had been the closest of shaves.

The three men remounted their animals and continued through the mountain gorge. By now it was half past six and getting to be dusk, which helped them in the sense that any further helicopter patrols would find it almost impossible to spot them. But on the other hand, traveling at night through the mountains seemed a daunting prospect, although it didn't seem to bother the sure-footed mules.

Johnson was very certain that if they hadn't had the early warning from whoever had tipped off Javed about the KGB, they would now be in some KHAD prison cell.

After seeing the black cars pull up outside the safe house,

it crossed Johnson's mind that Javed may have deliberately created some kind of delay—which certainly would have dire consequences for him with the KGB—to allow them to get away.

Maybe that somehow explained how Rostov had ended up pursuing them single-handed, with no obvious sign of backup. Otherwise, it seemed completely out of character for a high-level KGB officer to operate on the street alone. Not that Johnson was going to waste his energy trying to work out how that had happened.

It might also have explained how they had a clear run back across the river in the boat and then in the pickup back through the Goshta District. Johnson had been fully expecting them to come under fire or to be pulled over by security patrols. But it hadn't happened. Clearly if Javed were still alive, he had kept his mouth shut.

Also unexpected was the long period of time that had elapsed before helicopter patrols appeared on the route back through the Goshta District toward the safety of the Mohmand Agency and Pakistani territory.

It crossed Johnson's mind that the lack of military activity might be another sign that Russian forces were backing off in Afghanistan.

Unlike the route in, there was going to be no time for an overnight sleep stop. Despite the situation, Johnson had a couple of times found his eyelids drooping. He craved a coffee, and Vic and Elam were also both visibly exhausted.

After another forty-five minutes, with a three-quarter moon now lighting their path, they arrived back at the hut where the Toyota pickup was hidden, still intact in the shed. Johnson stopped and gazed at the bridge next to it, with its carved wooden eagles silhouetted in the moonlight. The place where Robert Watson had covertly handed over Stinger missiles to some unknown mujahideen. He had an urgent desire to photograph the scene but knew that in the darkness and without a flash he would be wasting his time.

Johnson remained as tense as a coiled spring. The question remained, could they trust Elam to now get them back over the border unscathed?

But getting this close to safety, Johnson began to allow himself to think through other issues.

"How are we going to play this with Watson?" he asked Vic as they bounced from one side of the moving Toyota to the other.

He grabbed the door handle as the Toyota hit a hole in the track and lurched sharply to the left. Elam, at the wheel, was battling to keep the vehicle on course without switching on his headlights.

"Good question," Vic said. "We'll struggle without that photo. It even pinned down the location of the handover. Why the hell Javed wouldn't just give it to us, I just don't know."

"He was panicked at the end. I'm sure if the meeting had gone the distance, we could have talked him into letting us keep it," Johnson said.

"There's also the question of who leaked the meeting to the KGB," Vic said. "Javed was insistent it wasn't at his end."

"If not, it has to have been on ours," Johnson said. "Watson again? The other thing is the fifty thousand bucks— what happened to that? Some KGB crook probably pocketed it."

Vic threw up his hands. "Screwed if I know, but we do know Watson's a moneygrubbing bastard, and if he's been selling Stingers privately to the muj, then frankly, he could be up to anything. Do you think he might be on the KGB payroll?"

Johnson shrugged. "A few days ago I'd have said that idea was a nonstarter. Now? I'm not so sure."

CHAPTER TWENTY-SEVEN

Monday, March 14, 1988
   Islamabad

Someone brought two bottles of champagne and a tray of glasses into the CIA secure meeting room, and a plastic model of an Mi-24 helicopter appeared on the table.

But Johnson wasn't in the mood for celebrating. Yes, he had played the key role in securing a Hind helicopter for the technical teams back at Langley to crawl over and suck out every last drop of Russian know-how. With President Zia's approval, the remains of the chopper were being dismantled and collected by a US transport aircraft and, as hoped, the weaponry, the cockpit, and the core technology all had remained intact. It was a highly valuable prize.

Watson had already received a congratulatory cable from Director Meyer, according to Alec Jameson, although so far there had been no sight of the station chief. "This success has just saved the Pentagon millions of dollars in research and development costs," the cable said.

Meyer had a meeting arranged for later in the week on Capitol Hill to brief the two skeptical Democratic senators, Rudder and Kendall. The hope was that the Hind triumph would be sufficient to tilt decisions on the Afghan program budget in the Agency's favor, at least for the next year, Jameson added.

One of the CIA's moles inside the Kremlin had also confirmed the death of Rostov from a gunshot wound. In contrast to Johnson, who cringed upon hearing the news, most of those in the Islamabad CIA station seemed privately delighted, not that they could even mention that outwardly. Jameson visibly struggled to keep the smirk off his face when Johnson recounted the story of what had happened. The Russian had been a large thorn in the CIA's flesh for a long time.

But news that Johnson had lost his agent, Javed, had come as a hammerblow. Within an hour of Johnson arriving back in Islamabad, and just after he had finished a brief call to Jayne to update her, Haroon had gotten in touch via burst radio. The ISI officer had picked up from sources inside the KHAD that Javed had been captured at the safe house by the KGB officer Severinov—the same man who had coordinated the gunship raid on Hani village—and had been taken to Pul-e-Charkhi prison for interrogation. Javed's partner had somehow escaped as the KGB closed in.

Johnson felt his guts turn over when he heard that news. There was only one likely outcome for Javed, given what he knew of KGB interrogation techniques at the prison.

Separately, Dennis Clarke had finally returned from his business trip, had had his basement swept for bugs, and had found a listening device in a ceiling light fitting that, from his description on the phone, sounded virtually identical to the ones that Johnson and Jayne had discovered hidden in their apartments three weeks earlier. The problem was, none of them could be certain about who had planted them. Johnson now could not escape the sneaking suspicion that it might well have been Watson rather than the ISI or the KGB—or even Jameson, as he had initially thought. Certainly, the use of different technology from the normal equipment used by the KGB and the ISI pointed in that direction.

What had further deepened the mystery was that Watson's secretary Pauline had refused to disclose to Johnson the name of the tall man from Kay Associates whom he had seen at the CIA station and who was in the background in the photograph that Javed and Baz had shown him. When Johnson approached her later, Pauline said that Watson had ordered her to keep the man's identity completely confidential, and there were no written records of it. That simply stiffened Johnson's resolve to find out who it was, although it would have to wait until another day.

It was now five o'clock in the afternoon. Johnson fingered the large white bandage that one of the doctors at the US embassy had put on his ear when he and Vic had finally made it back to the compound earlier that afternoon. There were some signs of infection in the wound, but the doctor cleaned and treated it and put Johnson on a course of antibiotics. The one thing he couldn't do was replace the small chunk of flesh that had disappeared.

Johnson turned back to Jameson. "What will the Russians do regarding Rostov, do you think?" It had been worrying him for the whole of the journey back to Islamabad. It seemed unthinkable to Johnson that killing a KGB officer, even in self-defense, would be something the Russians would allow to slip past without repercussions.

The deputy station chief pressed his lips and looked away. "Was he dead when you left him?"

"No, but obviously heading in that direction."

"Well, I don't know what the Russians will do. We'll find

out in the next day or two. Look, you were just doing your job, and it was a case of kill or be killed, from what you've told me. Try not to worry about it—think about the Hind." He gestured toward the plastic model on the table beside him. "You did a great job with that."

A few seconds later, the door to the meeting room opened and Watson came in. He glanced around and then headed straight toward Johnson and Jameson.

"Glad you made it back," Watson said, "and well done on the Hind. Langley is very happy. The director is grinning like a pig in shit with that."

"Thank you," said Johnson. He wanted to say a lot more but kept his mouth shut. *Let Watson do the talking for now.*

"However," Watson said, "I also have some bad news. I've had Gul on the phone twice in the past few hours. The first time was to confirm he was happy for us to take the Hind, and he said he hoped it helps us against the Russians. The second time, two hours later, he was incandescent with rage after finding out about the Jalalabad operation."

Watson stopped and surveyed Johnson, who again felt the bottom drop out of his stomach.

General Hamid Gul was the director-general of the ISI and one of President Zia's right-hand men. Watson had regular meetings with Gul as part of attempts to coordinate intelligence gathering and the dispersion of CIA weaponry to the mujahideen. Johnson knew that Watson had regularly reassured Gul that the CIA was not carrying out its own cross-border operations into Afghanistan, as instructed, and was doing everything through the ISI.

What an asshole hypocrite Watson is, Johnson thought.

"Right," Johnson said. "What's Gul saying?"

"His only concern is looking good in front of Zia. So he's going to call for a major inquiry into how CIA officers came to be over the border. He wants blood, basically."

Johnson exhaled. "What does that mean for me?"

Watson looked down at the model Mi-24 on the table. "What it means is that I'm going to have to find you something else to do—for the time being. I don't know what yet, but nothing to do with Afghanistan. You're off that program, effective immediately."

He glanced back up at Johnson. "You've worked asshole-fashion. I'm not going to support you over this."

* * *

Tuesday, March 15, 1988
Islamabad

Johnson woke just as the sun was rising at around six o'clock and turned his head. He was almost surprised to find she was still there—Jayne Robinson was lying faceup next to him, still asleep, covered by a sheet and a blanket. Her dark hair contrasted with the white pillow, and her breasts rose and fell rhythmically as she breathed. She looked beautiful like that.

He smiled to himself. He had felt utterly exhausted the previous evening when he had gotten back to his apartment and had fallen asleep on his sofa, only to be woken at ten o'clock by the door buzzer. Jayne had given him no option: he had to let her in.

By half past ten, reenergized just enough by a swiftly made espresso and a bar of chocolate, they were making love. It was as if the frustration and the anger and—he had to say —the wonder that he was still alive and back to tell the tale were poured into that hour before he fell once again into unconsciousness.

Johnson sank back into his pillow and stared at the ceiling.

Had it all been simply a result of pent-up emotions from the two highly dangerous operations he had been involved in? Was it because they had been thrown together in a high-pressure environment with little other social stimulation? Could there be more to it than that? Possibly. He liked her a lot, but he still felt he didn't know her very well, and he also still knew it wasn't sensible for either of them in terms of their work situations.

Stop analyzing and enjoy the moment, he told himself. He always overthought everything when it came to relationships.

Since they had kissed on his sofa five days earlier, before the Jalalabad trip, it had seemed almost inevitable that this was going to happen. But given the doubts at the back of his mind, he had still been surprised at how badly he had wanted her. The feeling had appeared to be mutual: they were in each other's arms within seconds of her walking through the door, after hardly exchanging a word.

Now he slowly climbed out of bed and pulled on his bathrobe, his head still dull with tiredness, but he knew there was no chance of sleeping any further. He had too many thoughts buzzing around in his head.

He quietly shut the bedroom door behind him and walked through to the kitchen. Like most of the diplomatic and intelligence service officers living in Islamabad, Johnson was well supplied with internal analysis of political events in the region. But he also invariably listened to either Voice of America or the BBC World Service radio news to keep himself up to date with the mainstream media perspective too.

He flicked on the radio, turned the sound down to a whisper, and tuned to the BBC, just in time for the start of the world news.

It was the fourth item that did it. The newsreader, in his

modulated British tones, didn't need to underline the gravity
of the situation.

> *"In Moscow, the Soviet Union has accused the United States
> of blatantly interfering in the Afghanistan conflict after a
> KGB intelligence service officer was apparently shot dead in
> Jalalabad, allegedly by a CIA officer working illegally in the
> country. According to an official spokesman at the Kremlin,
> the unnamed KGB officer was killed when he approached a
> CIA officer, also unnamed, who was in Jalalabad for a
> covert meeting with members of the mujahideen, who are
> fighting against the occupation of Afghanistan by the Soviet
> Union. The CIA and the US Department of Defense both
> declined to comment on the Soviet allegations. Mujahideen
> fighters have shot down several Soviet helicopters in
> Afghanistan over recent months, allegedly using US-made
> Stinger missiles. Most recently, three helicopters were report-
> edly downed on the border between Afghanistan and the
> Kurram Agency in northwest Pakistan on Wednesday last
> week. Despite Soviet leader Mikhail Gorbachev's promises to
> withdraw from Afghanistan, the country remains a major
> theater in the broader Cold War conflict between the two
> superpowers."*

Johnson felt a wave of anxiety flow through him. His fore-
head began to sweat. This was all getting out of hand. Langley
was bound to react strongly now that the news was being
broadcast across the globe, and the one man he needed to
back him was the same man who he suspected might possibly
have leaked details of his Hani and Jalalabad meetings to the
Russians, as well as have sold Stingers privately to some
mujahideen.

But the proof of the latter offense lay in the hands of
Javed, who was now apparently in Pul-e-Charkhi prison. And

Johnson had no proof of the former at all, beyond some sort of gut feeling.

On top of all that, the Pakistanis were on the warpath because he had gone cross-border against their explicit instructions but on the instructions of his boss. He just hoped for Haroon's sake that his covert role in the saga would not come to light.

He walked to the apartment window and gazed out across the city toward the green undulating slopes of the Margalla Hills to the northeast.

"Shit, shit, *shit*," he muttered to himself. This job—and this particular operation—had been so full of loose ends and unresolved anomalies. It felt as though his triumph in securing a Hind had already faded into the distant past.

"Morning, Joe," came a voice from behind him. He turned to see Jayne standing in the doorway, his spare blue robe wrapped around her.

She was smiling at him, but then she saw the expression on his face. "What's happening? Are you okay?"

Johnson walked over and kissed her gently, then put a hand on each of her shoulders.

"I was okay until I heard the news. It's all going to crap," Johnson said. He told her about the BBC bulletin.

"I don't know about this job anymore," Johnson said. He walked to the other side of the kitchen and leaned against the countertop. "I joined the Agency with ideas about working against the evil empire. Remember when Reagan put that tag on Russia a few years ago?"

"I remember it well," Jayne said.

"Well, that's what fired me up. I throw myself into it and take on jobs that are difficult and dangerous. Both the Hani and Jalalabad operations were life-on-the-line stuff. But then it turns out that there's an evil empire of a different kind much closer to home as well. And they put you through the wringer and then hang you out to dry when it all goes wrong. Maybe I should find something else to do."

Behind them, the BBC news broadcast continued. The final item in the bulletin was also about Afghanistan.

"From Afghanistan, news is coming in of a rocket attack on the Pul-e-Charki prison in Kabul, which the occupying Soviet forces and the Afghan regime use to hold mujahideen prisoners who have been accused or convicted of fighting against the Soviets. Initial reports suggest the rocket attack was carried out by mujahideen rebel forces, but that has not been confirmed. So far we have no details on the damage done or on casualties, but we will bring you more on that story in our next bulletin."

Johnson put his head in his hands.

"That doesn't sound good," Jayne said.

"No, especially if Javed was caught up in that. If he's now been killed in a rocket attack by his own people, after what he's just been through, well . . . " His voice trailed off.

Jayne walked to Johnson and hugged him. "Don't think the worst until you know," she said. "And as for your job, just don't jump to conclusions. Maybe this will all just blow over. These things happen in our line of work all the time. We're right in the firing line."

Johnson glanced at the radio. The BBC announcer was moving onto a news analysis program, which he said would be focused on the Afghanistan situation. "I don't think this is going to blow over very quickly," Johnson said, grimly.

EPILOGUE

Friday, September 23, 1988
  Portland, Maine

The front door opened slowly, and Helena Johnson's head appeared around the edge. Her mouth dropped open. "Joe, what are you doing here?"

"It's a long story, Mother. I've been fired."

"*Fired?* What are you talking about?"

"Yes," Johnson said. "They told me yesterday morning. Come on, let's go inside. I'll tell you what I can of what happened."

Johnson followed his sixty-three-year-old mother into the red-tiled hallway of the family house. As soon as she had closed the door, she grasped him in a tight hug, then stood back, one hand on each of his shoulders.

"Did you upset your boss? I know you said once he was difficult," she asked in her hybrid accent, New England mixed with a heavy dose of her native Polish. "Come on, I'll make you a coffee. You're looking exhausted."

"Well, yes. My boss was part of it," Johnson said as they walked through to the kitchen. "There was a lot more to it than that, though." There was no way he could go into details with his mother about a highly classified, deeply sensitive incident such as the Rostov shooting.

Helena switched on the kettle and took a French press and two cups from the cupboard. "Well, tell me, then."

She listened as Johnson described in extremely vague language how a project he was working on had gone wrong.

"Was it more serious than what you're suggesting?" Helena asked, looking at him suspiciously. He had always struggled to pull the wool over her eyes.

"Well, yes. I just can't go into details. Let's just say I was in a very difficult position and my boss hung me out to dry," Johnson said.

Helena poured hot water into the press and shook her head. "And that was the reason they fired you?"

"It was also partly because of Jayne." He had briefly mentioned the relationship to his mother a few months earlier, omitting the detail that she worked for MI6. "My boss found out about that and used it as an excuse."

"He can't fire you for having a girlfriend, can he?"

Johnson pressed his lips together. "No. It was more complicated than that. But I can't talk about that much, either."

After the Jalalabad incident, Watson had transferred Johnson off Afghanistan operations and onto a team collating intelligence on the Pakistani nuclear program. However, someone—probably Jameson, he suspected—had subsequently made Watson aware of Johnson's relationship with Jayne, and he had exploded. After a verbal and a written warning, his boss eventually had him recalled to Langley.

"How can he use a relationship as an excuse," Helena said. "It didn't interfere with your work, did it?"

"No. But that made no difference. Listen, I probably made a mistake," Johnson said. "All I can tell you is she's an intelligence officer for the British, and I guess in theory there was potentially a conflict there, the possibility of compromising operations. I mean, in practice, it never happened and never would. We were very professional about it. But it was the perception they had. What could I do? I was attracted to her, and sometimes you get attracted to people you shouldn't. You can't turn it off and on like a tap, can you?"

"True," Helena said, folding her arms. "Was it serious—with Jayne?"

"I like her a lot. I don't know if we'd be right for each other longer term. It was an odd environment there, and we worked together in a difficult situation—she saved my skin, actually. Maybe that was part of the attraction." He wasn't going to give his mother precise details of the hair-raising helicopter exfil operation that had extracted him from Hani.

"You used to talk about Kathy."

"Yes, I still keep in touch, vaguely. But she's in DC now. I haven't seen her for a long time."

Helena shrugged and pressed down the plunger in the press.

He had left Islamabad with a lot of unresolved issues and loose ends. There had been little time to work out things with Jayne and determine what they should do in terms of their relationship. There seemed little alternative but to agree to keep in touch and see each other again when they could. She definitely didn't want to throw away her career and therefore needed to remain in Islamabad, whereas he couldn't return there. They had spoken on the phone a few times since, but to Johnson, it seemed unworkable.

There was also the fate of Javed. After being thrown into Pul-e-Charkhi, was the mujahideen leader alive or dead? It was something that bothered Johnson deeply.

Neither had Johnson been able to find out—and now probably never would—whether Watson had actually leaked the details of the Hani and Jalalabad meetings to the Russians. He and Vic had both seen evidence of Watson's corruption on what looked like a large scale, but without a copy of the photograph of him handing over the Stingers to the mujahideen, how could he prove it to senior management at Langley? They would never believe him—Watson was too highly regarded on the seventh floor.

Johnson promised himself that one day, he would return to Afghanistan and try to find answers to those questions.

Once he had been sent back to Langley, Johnson knew it was only a matter of time. Sure enough, he had been called for a meeting with his departmental head the previous afternoon, just a couple of days after his thirtieth birthday, and told he was no longer required. He had been allowed to collect his belongings and was then escorted by security off the premises.

Four years after joining the CIA, he had lost his job.

"What are you going to do?" Helena asked. "Can you appeal? Take legal action?"

Johnson shook his head. "No, I don't want to. I'm done with the CIA. It was interesting while it lasted, but frankly, the enthusiasm, the passion I had when I joined has gone. I need to find something else."

Helena shook her head and gazed at her son. "What I have learned in life is that sometimes when one door closes, another opens."

"I'm sure you're right," Johnson said, "but now it doesn't feel like that."

Helena poured coffee into the two cups and pushed one across the counter to her son. She reached behind her and picked up a newspaper, flicking over the pages until she reached the careers section.

"Here, I was just reading that yesterday," Helena said. "I found it interesting. The Office of Special Investigations in Washington is looking for people to train and work as investigators—they're Nazi hunters for the government."

"Nazi hunters?" Johnson said. "I can see why you noticed it, but is that going to be right for me?"

"Maybe. They need people who are historians, with strong language skills, good at analysis, who are persistent, and so on. Have a look. It's inside the Department of Justice. Sounds as though the job description were written for you."

She tossed the newspaper across to Johnson, who glanced at it.

"War crimes investigator. Looks interesting, yes. But I'm going to take some time to think about what I want to do next. I'm not going to rush into anything."

His mother was indefatigable, always looking forward, always chasing the next opportunity and trying to get him to do the same. It was the attitude that had gotten her through two years in Hitler's concentration camps and then to the United States. If there was one thing he'd learned from her, it was to not dwell on the past or what had gone wrong and instead always move onward.

Helena reached for the sugar bowl. "You need to remember something my father always used to say," she said, picking up her spoon. "Sometimes the bad things turn out for good, the good things can never be lost, and usually, the best is yet to come."

She was right. Maybe he would just apply for that OSI job. Perhaps chasing war criminals might be something he'd love doing. And it was in DC. Johnson sipped his coffee and smiled for the first time in several days.

* * *

OTHER BOOKS IN THE SERIES AND READER UPDATES

Thank you for reading **The Afghan** — hopefully you enjoyed it. This is a prequel for the entire **Joe Johnson** series of thrillers, which are set in the present day and in which Joe is no longer a CIA officer, but an independent war crimes investigator, making full use of the skills he has learned at the Agency and subsequently as a Nazi hunter for the United States Department of Justice. In order, the books are:

1. *The Last Nazi*
2. *The Old Bridge*
3. *Bandit Country*
4. *Stalin's Final Sting*
5. *The Nazi's Son*

It makes sense to read the books in order, although the stories are all quite separate. You will find that some of the storylines that occur in **The Afghan** are developed and resolved during the other books, particularly in **Stalin's Final Sting**, which is also set mainly in Afghanistan with some key scenes in Moscow and New York City.

Work on a fifth book in the series is currently underway.

You can buy all the books in the series from Amazon — just go to the Amazon website, type "Andrew Turpin Joe Johnson thriller series" in the search box at the top, and you can't miss the books!

If you enjoyed this book, I would like to keep in touch. This is not always easy, as I usually only publish a couple of books a year and there are many authors and books out there. So the best way is for you to be on my Readers Group email list. I can then send you updates on the next book, plus occasional special offers.

If you are not already in my Readers Group and would like

to receive the email updates, you can sign up at the following link and I will send you a free taster ebook boxset containing the first few chapters of the other books in the series, including ***Stalin's Final Sting***:

https://bookhip.com/DGWGVP

If you only like paperbacks, you can still just sign up for the email list at the link above.

* * *

IF YOU ENJOYED THIS BOOK PLEASE WRITE A REVIEW

As an independently published author, through my own imprint The Write Direction Publishing, I find that honest reviews of my books are the most powerful way for me to bring them to the attention of other potential readers.

As you'll appreciate, unlike the big international publishers, I can't take out full-page advertisements in the newspapers or place posters on the subway.

So I am committed to producing work of the best quality I can in order to attract a loyal group of readers who are prepared to recommend my work to others.

Therefore, if you genuinely enjoyed reading this novel, then I would very much appreciate it if you would spend five minutes and leave a review—which can be as short as you like—preferably on the page or website where you bought it.

You can find the book's page on the Amazon website by typing 'Andrew Turpin The Afghan' in the search box.

Once you are on the book's page, scroll down to 'Customer Reviews', then click on 'Leave a Review.'

Reviews are also a great encouragement to me to write more!

Many thanks.

THANKS AND ACKNOWLEDGEMENTS

Thank you to everyone who reads my books. You are the reason I began to write in the first place, and I hope I can provide you with entertainment and interest for a long time into the future.

I really do enjoy having contact with my readers. Every time I get an encouraging email, or a positive comment on my Facebook page, or a nice review on Amazon, it spurs me on to press ahead with my research or writing for the next book. So keep them coming!

Specifically with regard to **The Afghan**, there are several people who have helped me during the long process of research, writing, and editing.

I have two editors who consistently provide helpful advice, food for thought, great ideas, and constructive criticism, and between them have enabled me to considerably improve the initial draft. Katrina Diaz Arnold, owner of Refine Editing, again gave me a lot of valuable feedback at the structural and line levels, and Jon Ford, as ever, helped me to maintain the authenticity of the story in many areas through his great eye for detail. I would like to thank both of them—the responsibility for any remaining mistakes lies solely with me.

As always, my brother, Adrian Turpin, has been a very helpful reader of my early drafts and highlighted areas where I need to improve. Others, such as Martin Scales, David Cole, David Payne, and Warren Smith have done likewise. The small but dedicated team in my Advance Readers group went through the final version prior to proofreading and also highlighted a number of issues that required changes and improvements—a big thank you to them all.

I would also like to thank the team at Damonza for what I think is a great cover design.

AUTHOR'S NOTE

The conflict in Afghanistan during and after the Soviet military occupation from 1979 to 1989 has been a rich feeding ground for fiction and nonfiction authors alike.

As with all the books in the Joe Johnson war crimes series, much of the historical backdrop to *The Afghan* is factual, including details of the atrocities inflicted on the Afghan population during that time.

The Khost-Gardez Pass was the scene of many bloody battles during that period between the Soviet army and the mujahideen forces who managed for almost all of those ten years to control the pass and keep them at bay.

In particular, the deployment by the Soviets of Mil Mi-24 helicopters—dubbed Hinds by NATO—and the use by the mujahideen of Stinger missiles to combat them has become the stuff of legend.

During all of this, the ongoing duels between the Soviet intelligence service, the KGB, on one side, and the CIA, MI6, and Pakistan's ISI, who were supporting the mujahideen on the other side, were critical to the outcome.

As with all the books in this series, because my protagonist Joe Johnson is from the United States, and most scenes are from his point of view, it seemed to make sense to try to use American spellings and terminology wherever possible, rather than my native British.

RESEARCH AND BIBLIOGRAPHY

My research for *The Afghan* and for its direct sequel in the Joe Johnson series, *Stalin's Final Sting*, was all carried out as part of the same process. Both books are set mainly in Afghanistan and I researched, wrote, and edited both of them in parallel. The biggest difference lies in the timeframe: *The Afghan* is set in 1988, when Johnson was still working for the CIA, and *Stalin's Final Sting* in 2013, but there are many references in the latter book to events and situations in the former.

For this reason, the following notes that I have put together on my research sources are very similar for both titles.

Across both books the research proved to be so interesting that I often found myself immersed in some book or article online and had to remind myself to get on with it, collect the information I needed, and focus on the writing of my story.

The whole saga of the Soviet occupation of Afghanistan really is a classic case study of the CIA at work to try to further the interests of the United States in an under-the-radar manner. As the Soviet army marched in during December 1979, the Cold War was running strongly, and there is no doubt that the US feared what the next move would be if it proved successful.

As it happened, the Soviets ended up being bogged down in an attritional war against the mujahideen that lasted for nine years before they finally pulled out in 1989—just before the Eastern European revolutions of that year, including the fall of the Berlin Wall, that led to the collapse of the Soviet Union.

That certainly did not seem the likely outcome during the

first few years of the occupation, when over 100,000 Soviet troops took control of Afghanistan, backed by the KGB.

The CIA, which together with Pakistan's ISI intelligence agency assisted the mujahideen in their fight, can take a large amount of credit for the eventual victory.

The CIA's Operation Cyclone proved a critical turning point. This program funded and arranged the supply of Stinger missiles from September 1986 onward, which finally gave the mujahideen the weaponry they needed to combat the terrifying Soviet Mil Mi-24 gunship helicopters—dubbed the "Hind" by NATO.

These Hinds had been used by the Soviets to destroy villages and to kill a lot of the two million Afghans who died during the war. Another three million fled the carnage across the border into Pakistan.

Anyone who would like a colorful and racy account of how the Stingers were deployed by the CIA, and the politics behind those decisions, should look no further than *Charlie Wilson's War*, by George Crile, available on Amazon.

A 2007 film of the book, under the same title, and starring Tom Hanks and Julia Roberts, is also available. There is no doubt that the late Charlie Wilson, a Democratic congressman, was a driving force that championed the use of Stingers and cajoled and pushed his colleagues in Congress to support Operation Cyclone with ever-increasing levels of funding. It seems likely that without the energy of this larger-than-life character, they may not have been deployed at all.

Another extremely insightful book is *Ghost Wars*, by Steve Coll, a *Washington Post* journalist. The book covers the CIA's operations in Afghanistan from 1979 through to 2001 and includes sections on Bin Laden. It is available on Amazon.

Milton Bearden, a thirty-year CIA veteran, was station chief in Islamabad from 1986–89, during which time he was very heavily involved in Operation Cyclone. He subsequently wrote a vivid and technically detailed thriller about the battles between the Soviets and the mujahideen entitled *The Black Tulip* (1998), which is still available on Amazon. I found it very useful as background reading and as an inspiration for some of my plot lines.

Before anyone asks, my fictional CIA Islamabad station chief during the 1980s, Robert Watson, is NOT based on Bearden, who I'm sure would be appalled at most of the things Watson did during his career.

For more color about the impact of the Soviet occupation on the Afghan people, I would recommend a book by ITN journalist Sandy Gall, *Agony of a Nation* (1988) which is available on Amazon.

On the genocide committed by Soviet forces against the Afghan population, there is a good article by Michael Reisman and Charles Norchi that details the extent of depopulation and atrocities committed. Entitled "Genocide and the Soviet Occupation of Afghanistan," it can be found at: http://www.paulbogdanor.com/left/afghan/genocide.pdf.

A good summary of the Soviet-Afghan war, including the extent of the genocide perpetrated by Soviet forces, can be found in Wikipedia, at: https://en.wikipedia.org/wiki/Soviet%E2%80%93Afghan_War#Destruction_in_Afghanistan.

The legendary Khost-Gardez Pass may need little introduction. However, there are some excellent videos on YouTube about this region, including a few about the lengthy and controversial construction project to pave the highway. For example, there is this one produced by USAid: https://www.youtube.com/watch?v=-ciitRebvuA, and another by the same organization: https://www.youtube.com/watch?v=pdYAR3C6uJg.

These two films give a good illustration of the type of terrain through which the highway passes and the small villages en route, similar to my fictional village of Wazrar. I could have chosen a real village as the backdrop for the scenes in the K-G Pass, but I decided that the sensitivities of the situations I was writing about made it perhaps better to come up with a fictional one, albeit closely based on reality.

These books, articles, and videos are simply a flavor of the many I read and watched while researching *Stalin's Final Sting* and *The Afghan*. However, they do give you the basis for some further reading should you be so inspired.

ABOUT THE AUTHOR AND CONTACT DETAILS

I have always had a love of writing and a passion for reading good thrillers. But despite having a long-standing dream of writing my own novels, it took me more than five decades to finally get around to completing the first.

The Afghan is a prequel to the **Joe Johnson** series of thrillers that pulls together some of my other interests, particularly history, world news, and travel.

I studied history at Loughborough University and worked for many years as a business and financial journalist before becoming a corporate and financial communications adviser with several large energy companies, specializing in media relations.

Originally I came from Grantham, Lincolnshire, and I now live with my family in St. Albans, Hertfordshire, U.K.

You can connect with me via these routes:

E-mail: andrew@andrewturpin.com
Website: www.andrewturpin.com.
Facebook: @AndrewTurpinAuthor
Twitter: @AndrewTurpin
Instagram: @andrewturpin.author

Please also follow me on Bookbub and Amazon!

https://www.bookbub.com/authors/andrew-turpin
https://www.amazon.com/Andrew-Turpin/e/B074V87WWL/

Do get in touch with your comments and views on the books, or anything else for that matter. I enjoy hearing from readers and promise to reply.